K. L. Going

Harcourt, Inc.

Orlando   Austin   New York   San Diego   London

Requests for permission to make copies of any part of the work
should be submitted online at www.harcourt.com/contact or mailed
to the following address: Permissions Department, Harcourt, Inc.,
6277 Sea Harbor Drive, Orlando, Florida 32887-6777.

www.HarcourtBooks.com

Library of Congress Cataloging-in-Publication Data
Going, K. L. (Kelly L.)
The garden of Eve/K. L. Going.
p. cm.
Summary: Eve gave up her belief in stories and magic
after her mother's death, but a mysterious seed given her as an
eleventh-birthday gift by someone she has never met takes her
and a boy who claims to be a ghost on a strange journey, to where
their supposedly cursed town of Beaumont, New York, flourishes.
[1. Seeds—Fiction. 2. Magic—Fiction. 3. Orchards—Fiction. 4. Death—
Fiction. 5. Grief—Fiction. 6. Family life—New York (State)—Fiction.
7. New York (State)—Fiction.] I. Title.
PZ7.G559118Gar 2007
[Fic]—dc22 2007005074
ISBN 978-0-15-205986-6

Text set in ITC Legacy Serif Book
Designed by Linda Lockowitz

First edition
A C E G H F D B

Printed in the United States of America

Contents

For Kyle, who said,
"Write a story about an apple tree…"

Prelude

nce there was a beautiful garden."

"Like our garden?"

"Almost, but so much bigger."

"Were there trees? Like Father grows? Or just fruits and vegetables?"

"Every kind of tree grew in the garden. There were maple trees and oak trees. Fig trees and olive trees. There were orange trees and..."

"Apple trees!"

"Yes, apple trees."

"What kind of animals were there?"

"Oh, more than I could name before bedtime. Let's see. There were tigers and rhinoceroses and brilliant white unicorns..."

"Unicorns aren't real. Father said so. He says none of your stories are true, because if magic were real you wouldn't be sick."

"Is that what Father says? Well, I'll tell you a secret, but you musn't tell anyone else."

"What secret?"

"Father doesn't know everything. He doesn't even know enough to come inside for stories at night and that is very important, now isn't it?"

"Yes. Very."

"But you know what? Someday even Father might find a magical garden."

"Would he take us to see it?"

"He'd bring you, Evie. Father always remembers you, even when it seems like he's forgotten."

"And will he bring you, too?"

"Maybe. Or maybe I will already be there, waiting where the grass is green and the trees are always in bloom, and the cherry tree petals blow along on the wind like the rain."

"Mom? Was there really a Garden of Eden? Not a story, but an actual place?"

"That all depends on whether you believe. Some people say there was a real garden, but it withered up and blew away. Other people say it was a story. A few people think it still exists, but no one knows for sure."

"What do you think?"

"Me? I think a real garden would be pretty overgrown

by now, wouldn't it? So maybe someday we'll each find our own perfect garden instead."

"But how will we get there?"

"That's a good question. Maybe we can only go to our garden after we die. Perhaps that's why we're not allowed to live forever."

"Will you die?"

"Yes. We all will someday."

"Will you find a beautiful garden, Mom?"

"I hope so, Evie."

"Then I will meet you there. And I will bring Father with me even if he doesn't believe in perfect gardens and wants to weed instead."

"Okay, that's a good plan, but you should only come when it's the right time. Until then, help Father here with his garden. Promise?"

"Well . . ."

"You must."

"Okay. I promise."

But behind her back, Evie crossed her fingers.

Three years later...

CHAPTER ONE

The Fork in the Road

he final bend on the last road would take them to Beaumont. Father wanted to go straight but there was a fork in the road, so he stopped their old truck, packed full of their belongings, and got out to stare down each darkened, narrow lane. Maybe they were lost and they'd have to turn around and go home to Michigan.

Evie hoped they were lost.

She rolled down the window despite the cold. "Let's go back," she called, but as she said it Father took several steps forward and disappeared into the thick fog. Evie waited, and when he didn't answer she sat up straight in the front seat, her heart pounding in her chest. She pushed at the door, but just as it opened Father reappeared piece by piece, his solid figure emerging from the deep gray.

"Can't tell which way to go," he said, coming back to the truck and leaning on the edge of her open window. He was wearing his padded gardening jacket and thick leather gloves, but his cheeks were red and the skin around his beard was windburned already. Cold filled the truck. "Fog's too thick, and I sure don't remember there being a fork in the road."

He scratched his chin and took the crumpled directions from his jacket pocket. He'd gotten them months ago, before he'd visited the property, scribbling them onto the back of a grocery list because it had been nearest to the telephone. *Milk, eggs, peanut butter, whole wheat bread, take Route 71 east until you reach exit 7, then go 70 miles on Route 77....*

Evie brought her knees up to her chest and shivered in the late October air. Her pant legs rode up her ankles, letting the cold sting her bare skin. The pants were too short, but they were the last ones her mom would ever buy her—the last of her pretty clothes with no grass stains on the knees from rolling down hills or holes in the sides from catching on thorns. She wouldn't get rid of them no matter how small they got. She'd tried to stop growing instead, but it hadn't worked. Her legs were long and gangly, like a boy's.

Evie pulled her socks up as high as they would go and tugged at her winter coat to bring it lower. She peered down each road, only they both looked the same. Nothing but trees on every side, stretching as far as the eye could see—a thick forest between two great mountain ridges. The day was bleak, and the trees stood like sentries standing guard.

The truck door opened and Evie's father slid back into the driver's seat.

"I wrote down 'straight,'" he said, pointing toward the crumpled paper. "I'm certain it was straight until town. It's the strangest thing."

Evie twisted her hair into a curl, but it fell flat again as soon as she let go. Mom's had never done that. She sighed, and a flock of crows lifted up at once, as if released by her breath. They spiraled into the fog and their calls filled the air like a thunderous warning.

Evie shivered.

"We should go home," she said again. "We must have made a wrong turn."

She thought over the drive from Michigan to New York, and each turn seemed like a wrong turn. How could they move so far from Mom?

Everyone thought Father was making a mistake. *Everyone.* She'd heard them whispering, and no one had come to help them pack or see them off because Father wouldn't let them. Not even his own mother had been allowed over.

"I don't intend to take help from the same people who are talking behind my back," he'd told her, but it had felt awful to leave with only the neighbor next door waving from his front window. After that there'd been highway after highway and an overnight stay in a hotel that didn't have a TV and smelled like stale crackers.

Father had tried to say it was an adventure they were on, which wasn't like him at all, but Evie only scowled and stared out the window, occasionally kicking the dashboard. Adventures were things that Mom went on, not Father, and they didn't begin at five thirty in the morning with a stalled truck that took half an hour to start and empty roads going nowhere.

"This is all wrong," Evie muttered, but Father shook his head.

"Nah," he said, "this is it."

His dark eyes flashed the way they did when there was trouble to be figured out. They'd flashed that way the day he'd told her about buying the land. Only seven months after Mom died, he'd come to dinner all excited about a phone call from an old man.

"Fifty acres, Evie, and he's practically giving them away because the orchard hasn't been producing fruit.

People around there think it's a curse, but they're just superstitious, that's all." Father had paced around the kitchen, waving his arms as he spoke.

"They talk themselves into believing in curses and bad luck, but that's just foolishness. It was disease that made those trees sick and it's hard work that will make them better."

Evie didn't care whether the stupid trees got better. Why should trees get better when people didn't? Even the old man had died not long after that phone call. She'd crossed her fingers and toes that the deal would fall through, but it hadn't. The old man's sister had sold them the property instead, just as her brother had wished, and now three months later they were on their way.

Evie frowned and stared out the window.

"I hope we never get there," she mumbled, but Father just glanced across the front seat of the truck and sighed. He reached over and smoothed the hair from Evie's forehead. Her bangs hung in her eyes because Father never got around to cutting them—not even when Evie asked him to. *"Tomorrow,"* he always said. *"I've got a sick tree that needs attention, but I promise to do it tomorrow."*

Except tomorrow never came and now the scissors were packed along with everything else. Evie pulled away and Father put his hand back on the steering wheel.

"We're almost there," he said, real soft. "I'd guess another five miles will get us to Beaumont, provided we pick the right road." He paused, then looked over, catching Evie's eye.

"You pick, Evie."

Even now her stomach still turned somersaults. *"You pick, Tally."*

It was Mom's job to pick. Always had been. Father said she had a perfect sense of direction, but Mom always said the wind told her which way to go.

Evie could picture her mother getting out of the truck to inspect the fork where the roads met. She would stand still and tall, her spiraled hair pulled back in a headband. She'd be wearing the cargo pants Evie loved, with all the pockets in them, and the thick leather sandals she wore all year long, even in the winter. Then she'd wait, breathing long and full until she knew which choice to make.

"The answers are always out there, Evie," she used to say. *"You just have to wait until they whisper in your ear."*

Evie wanted to get out and stand in the exact spot where she'd pictured her mom standing. The wind was blowing strong and seemed to have something to say, as if *this* time when Evie stood still, she might hear something other than deafening silence. She wanted it so badly her insides stung like scraped knees on pavement, but already she could feel her muscles tightening and her ears closing until even the sound of the crows faded into the distance.

"Go on," Father nudged, but Evie shook her head.

Father's hands gripped the steering wheel. Then at last he turned the key in the ignition and the old truck rumbled to life. He breathed out long and loud until it seemed that all the air had escaped his lungs.

"Left it is then," he said at last. "One choice is as good as another."

CHAPTER TWO

∽

The Pale Boy

When they drove into the forest, Evie had a sudden desire for bread crumbs, just like Hansel and Gretel in the story that Mom used to read her before bed. The road twisted and turned. Pavement gave way to gravel and for a while the truck bumped along noisily. Then the trees on the left-hand side of the road dwindled and Father pointed ahead of them.

"There's the orchard."

Evie stared at the long, snaking lines of apple trees. They were dead, of course. Anyone who knew anything about Beaumont knew that. But the air still smelled strong, like earthy apple cider. As they drove forward branches reached out like bony arms, warning them back.

"Careful in the trees," Mom once said. *"There's more out there than your father's roots and vines. Magical things lurk beneath the branches…"*

But it had been ten months since Mom died and

there hadn't been anything magical at all—no beautiful gardens or answers carried on the wind. The world was as Father said it was. Soil + water + sunlight = life, and everything that lived also died and returned to the soil to start the cycle again.

Unless you were in Beaumont.

Here there didn't seem to be any life at all. Even the crows had stopped flying overhead and the wind ceased whistling through the branches. Father hit the radio button and it crackled on, but there was only static to break the silence, so he shut it off again and now it was quieter than quiet.

"Ought to be a sign soon," Father mumbled.

Evie scowled. Who would make a sign for a town that no one had cared about since the 1900s? Only there was a sign—an old wooden billboard along the side of the road. It said WELCOME TO BEAUMONT, in large swirly letters, and beneath it was written, HOME OF THE NEW YORK APPLE, with a picture of an apple in place of the word. The painted letters were cracked and faded into the weathered wood, but you could see what it might have looked like when the colors were bright and cheerful and the apple trees were alive and full of fruit.

"We're here," Father said. Evie looked around. There didn't seem to be anything *to* here. Just a long stretch of forest on one side and an abandoned house at the edge of the orchard on the other. From the looks of things, they'd be the only ones alive in all of Beaumont.

Except just at that moment they came upon the funeral.

The cemetery was on the left, set back from the road, not far from the old house. The gray head-stones blended into the sky, so that only the mourn-ers stood out. There was a small gathering of people dressed in black pants and stockings and long black overcoats all standing around what Evie knew must be a grave. Their hats and scarves were clutched tightly, but nothing moved, as if they were frozen in time, trapped by a wicked spell.

"Wonder who died," Father said aloud. He slowed the truck so that its engine didn't make such a loud clanging against the silence of the late afternoon. Evie pressed her face against the window. Her stom-ach twisted into a knot so tight she couldn't breathe. The day of Mom's funeral had been gray and bleak, just like this one. She turned away, but from the cor-ner of her eye she caught the movement of a figure stepping apart from the crowd.

Evie turned. The figure was a boy who looked to be about her own age, and he was the palest boy Evie had ever seen. His skin was ghostly white against the black of his coat and his pale hands were ungloved, making him appear as if hands and face were all there was to him.

The boy was the only one who noticed them and he turned to watch the truck as it crept past. No one else seemed to see him, and the look on his face was so stark and stricken with grief that Evie pressed her hand, fingers splayed, against the truck window.

"Do you see that boy…?" Evie started, but just as she spoke the boy turned and slid back into the crowd, swallowed up by a sea of black coats. Father glanced at the graveyard.

"Someone your age?"

Evie shrugged. What difference did that make? But for some reason she still strained to see him in the rearview mirror.

Father kept driving and the boy and the funeral disappeared completely. The road led into a small town, and shops began to pop up, lining each side of the street. There were twelve of them in all, but most were closed and some were boarded up as if they hadn't been open for a long time.

After the stores there was nothing but empty road as far as the eye could see. A sign on a lamppost read CLAIREVILLE 35, DUPONT 48. Thirty-five miles to the next-nearest town.

Evie frowned. They were passing a small park, but the jungle gym was rusted and the swings were broken. She concentrated on the buildings that still seemed to have life left in them—a grocery store, a bank, a little library....

Her eyes lingered on the library, and she remembered the way she and Mom used to race up the library steps back home.

"First one to find a book gets to pick the bedtime story!"

Only there were no bedtime stories now, and Father didn't even slow down as they passed. He pulled up in front of a small store on the opposite side of the road instead—one with rakes and a hay bale decorating the front window. Exactly the place Father would choose to stop.

"We need to go in for the key," he said, shutting off the engine. "Just a quick visit." The sign in the store window read CLAYTON'S FARM SUPPLIES.

Father went in and Evie followed reluctantly several feet behind him. Bells chimed loudly when they stepped inside, but no one answered them. In fact, there was no sign of anyone, which was just as well as far as Evie was concerned. Father craned his neck and stepped around one of the aisles.

"Do you think anyone's here?" he asked. Just then a door in the back opened and a large woman bustled out. She stopped and studied Father carefully but didn't seem to notice Evie hovering around the corner.

"Frank Adler?" she asked. "You look different from the day we closed on the house. Must be the beard." She chuckled. "Glad to see you made it. I've got the key around here somewhere."

She patted the pockets of a large apron.

"Good to see you again," Father said, reaching behind him to pull Evie forward. "This is my daughter, Evie."

The old woman froze.

"Your daughter?" she asked, her breath catching. "Her name is Eve?" She ignored Father's puzzled look. "You didn't tell me you had a daughter. I assumed you were a bachelor like my brother."

Evie rolled her eyes. That was typical of Father, to forget to mention her.

The woman clucked and shook her head. She was tall and sturdy and her long gray braid fell all the way to her waist. Evie wanted to dislike her because she was staring rudely, but for some reason she couldn't. Then suddenly, like a burst balloon, the woman laughed, and it was a loud, boisterous laugh that filled the room.

"Forgive me," she said. "I'm just so surprised!"

The truth was, she had a wonderful laugh—loud and ringing—and Evie couldn't help feeling tingly, as if she'd met this woman before someplace and they'd sat together in front of a fireplace having hot cocoa with marshmallows.

I don't care, Evie thought. *I still won't like her.*

"The name's Margaret," the woman said. "Although you can call me Maggie, like everyone else." She scooped Evie's hand into hers and her touch felt warm and soft like Gram's always felt, but Maggie didn't look as old as Gram. At least, not exactly. Her hair was gray, but it whipped as she turned her head, and her eyes were young and sparkly. She smiled at Evie.

"Beautiful," she said, as if making up her mind. Evie blushed. Then she frowned, keeping her arms crossed. She wasn't beautiful. That much she knew for certain. She was skinny and plain, with legs far too long for a ten-year-old girl.

Still, something about the way the old woman said "beautiful," so sure and final, made Evie wish she had a mirror, as if maybe she'd changed during the ride from Michigan to New York.

"I've been so excited for you to arrive," Maggie said, turning back to Father. "If I'd known you had a daughter, I would have cleaned the house up a bit more, but to be honest I haven't gone over there much since Rodney died."

"Sorry for your loss," Father said, shifting uncomfortably. Maggie just smiled again, and it was a sadder smile, but her eyes still twinkled.

"It's all right," Maggie said. "My brother lived a long life. He was ninety years old, you know. I suspect he's more at peace now than he ever was while he lived. Poor old Rodney never had much luck."

She sighed.

"I just wish he could have met you," she said, looking straight at Evie. "Although I suppose he must have known you were coming?" She glanced at Father.

"I probably mentioned Evie when we spoke on the phone," Father said, but he didn't sound sure at all. Evie pulled at a loose string on her coat, twisting it until it snapped.

Maggie clucked again. "Well…regardless, you're just what this town needs—people to till the soil again. Beaumont is going to have another heyday, you mark my words, and folks like us, folks with vision, why, we'll be the ones here to see it. Now isn't that right?"

Father nodded and shuffled his feet.

If Mom were here, she would have laughed and smiled and she and Maggie would have been best friends within the hour. Father only cleared his throat and Evie studied her torn sneakers. There was a long pause while Father tried to think of something new to say, and then he said something, but it was exactly the wrong thing.

"I see you've had a death in town. We drove past the funeral."

This time Maggie's smile faded completely.

"Yes," she said after a long moment. "A young boy passed away. Very sad. He was just ten years old."

Evie looked up. She hadn't meant to say anything, but now she couldn't help it.

"What did he die from?"

Maggie shook her head. "Leukemia. He died several days ago. Unfortunately they've got a frigid day for the funeral. We've been having a bad spat, you know. It's unseasonably cold considering it's not even November yet, but weather here tends toward the odd side. Something about being in the valley. The wind funnels through these mountains…"

Evie stopped listening. She thought of the pale face in the crowd of mourners. A boy about ten. But that boy had been alive. Only he hadn't looked alive, had he?

"…isn't that right, Evie?"

Father was asking her something, and Maggie was waiting expectantly for her to answer. When Evie didn't respond, Maggie's eyes widened.

"No school?" she said. "What will you do with yourself all day? Surely homeschooling can't be better than being in a classroom full of kids your own age to work with?"

Evie wanted to tell her that homeschooling was the way they'd always done things. The way Mom had set things up. She didn't care for a classroom full of kids her own age.

"I don't need any school," she said at last. "Father will teach me."

Maggie put her hand on Evie's head.

"Well," she said, "maybe you and your father will change your minds come winter. Beaumont's got a small school, but it's a good one. Plus, we've got a wonderful library across the street where you could meet people. I suspect that a girl your age will want some friends." She winked and something about her almost made Evie want to wink back, but Father reached over and took Evie's hand, engulfing it in his large calloused one.

"We should go," he said, but Evie was still thinking about the pale boy from the cemetery.

"That boy," she said at last, "the one who died. What was his name?"

Maggie's eyebrows arched.

"Eve," she said, "you'll be wanting live friends, I suspect." She paused. "You'll find folks in this town don't like to speak of the dead much. Beaumont's had more than its fair share of troubles." She paused again. "But," she said at last, taking out a small laminated card with a picture on it, "his name was Alex and this is his prayer card. The church gives them out so we'll remember to pray for the family. You can keep it if you'd like."

Evie took the card and studied the boy in the picture. It was hard to tell for sure, but Evie thought he looked like the boy she'd seen.

"Alex," she whispered.

She wanted to ask more, like where he had lived and what his family was like, but Father was nodding and glancing outside toward the truck like it was time to go. "It's a shame," he said, but his voice sounded far away, like he wasn't really thinking about the boy at all. "We should be getting on."

Maggie nodded. "Why don't I go over and show you around," she said, taking off her apron.

Father shook his head. "No need. I know where to find the place."

"Are you sure?" Maggie asked. "I could help you clean up a bit." She held the key out tentatively, and Father took it, thrusting it deep into his jacket pocket.

"We'll be fine," Father said in his "end of discussion" voice. "We don't need any help."

Evie glanced out the window at their truck, packed high with boxes that would soon need to be unpacked. She pulled her hand from Father's grip and Maggie's sharp eyes narrowed.

"I see…," she said. "Well, if you change your mind, you know where to find me. At least the funeral crowd will have cleared out by now." She laughed again and nodded at Evie. "Hope you're not frightened of cemeteries, my dear."

Evie's heart clenched tight. Cemeteries?

Father studied the floor and Maggie paused, looking back and forth between them.

"Didn't you know?" she asked. Maggie took one look at Evie's face and squeezed her shoulder tight. "Don't worry, love," she said. "I grew up in that house and I never saw a single ghost. And trust me, *I was watching.*"

CHAPTER THREE

The House by the Cemetery

vie's heart pounded as they pulled into the driveway of the old house with the peeling paint and broken shutters. Her fists clenched tight with fury. They couldn't live next to a cemetery. *Couldn't.* It wasn't even the *right* cemetery. Hot tears fought to escape, but she wouldn't let them.

"Evie, I…" Father turned the engine off and studied the steering wheel. "I meant to tell you. It's just…I wanted you to give this place a chance, and once we're inside you'll barely see the cemetery. We can pretend it isn't even there."

He waited for her response, and when she didn't answer he closed his eyes. "I'm sorry," he said. "I should have told you."

Mom would have told her. There was no doubt about that.

Evie crossed her arms over her chest. "I hate you,"

she said. "I'm not getting out. Ever. Not if I have to live next to a cemetery in a rotten old house."

Father's grip on the steering wheel tightened, and Evie almost wished he would yell at her, but he didn't. He got out and emptied the front seat of their soda pop cans and extra snack bags instead.

"You'll have to come inside sooner or later," he said when he'd finished. "It's too cold to stay out here for long." Then he shut the truck door extra hard and walked up to the house. Evie watched him fumble with the key, then lean his shoulder in to give the door a push. He went inside without looking back once.

Maybe he'd even forget she was there.

Evie swiped at her nose with her sleeve, then she studied the old house. Two cracked steps led up to a long front porch with chipped pillars. There were scraggly, barren bushes along the edge and a spindly tree in the front yard that had probably once been a cherry tree. She could tell from the bark and the shape of the branches. There was an old willow on the side of the house, and then the orchard, so close she felt as if she could almost touch the nearest apple trees.

But it wasn't the apple trees that finally drew Evie

out of the truck. It wasn't even the cold, which numbed her fingers and toes. It was her first glimpse inside.

Father had left the front door open, and just past it she could see a hallway with a picture hanging at the far end. Even from the truck she could see the painting clearly, framed between the banister and the wall. It was a portrait of an old man, hunched and wrinkled, but his blue eyes were bright and they seemed to stare straight at Evie. They were urgent, determined eyes, and something about them looked familiar. At first she thought it was because they looked like Maggie's eyes, but they didn't really. Yet they still looked like eyes she had seen before.

Evie waited a long while, but every time she looked back the eyes were calling her. She wished Father would shut the door, but he didn't, so finally she got out of the truck and moved carefully up the front steps. They creaked under her weight with an eerie whine.

I'll only stay a minute, she thought.

Evie stood gingerly under the low overhang of the front porch and studied the painting. She stepped inside and…

"You made it. See? It's not so bad in here." Father came around the corner and Evie jumped, but he didn't seem to notice. He reached out to trace the line of her cheek with one finger.

"I'm glad you came in," Father said, studying her carefully. "You're right. I should have told you about the cemetery. I just wanted you to see all the other great parts of this place without judging it first. It's like something out of those books you and your mom always read, don't you think?"

His face cracked into a smile, as if he couldn't quite help himself. Evie remembered when Father had smiled like this all the time, but that was over three years ago, back before Mom got sick and he started working in Farmer Dolan's orchard all the time. It was so long ago that she could hardly make it real anymore. Watching him now was like meeting someone on the street who you hadn't realized was missing—you felt all the pleasure of seeing them and all the pain of missing them at once.

He was wrong about the books though. Evie and Mom hadn't read stories about dusty old houses next to cemeteries. They'd read about beautiful gardens and magical lands with unicorns and castles....

Suddenly she missed their life in Michigan so bad it hurt. She pictured their house—the shelves full of books, the brightly colored paintings on every wall, and the pottery wheel in the back studio, where

Mom had been teaching her to mold clay. Every nook and cranny had held something interesting, and when Mom floated around in her long, flowing skirts and sandaled feet, it had been exactly where she belonged.

That was perfect. This house was cracked and worn, and there was no life to it whatsoever.

"I wish we'd stayed home," Evie said.

Father's smile faded.

"Well, we didn't. At least this house is furnished and paid for and there aren't a million reminders everywhere…"

Father ran his fingers through his thick hair. He closed his eyes, and Evie wondered if he would leave—maybe he'd go out to the orchard to work on the trees—but he didn't. Instead he sighed and took her by the shoulders.

"Try to imagine what this place might look like once we've fixed it up," he said, turning her in the direction of the large living room. "See this room?" There was furniture in it covered with sheets, and long windows with closed curtains.

"We'll add a new coat of paint on the walls and you can decorate the trim. We'll use some caulking to fill in those cracks, maybe clean up that fireplace and get the flue working, stack up some wood from outside…"

Father turned her across the hall toward the kitchen.

"We'll patch up those cabinets. Table and chairs are sturdy enough from the looks of them. If the oven works, we'll be making apple pies next fall—apple dumplings, apple cider… And outside, when the orchard comes back to life… Can't you see it, Evie?"

The truth was, she almost could, but she could also see the cemetery from the kitchen window, and just then she was certain she saw a figure walking through the rows of gravestones.

"No," she said, "I can't."

She slipped out of Father's grasp and ran back through the front door.

"Evie!" Father called after her, but she ignored him. Instead she walked outside, looking for the lonely figure, but he was already moving in the opposite direction. She could clearly see that it was the boy again, his dark shape fading into the distance, then disappearing entirely through the trees. Evie stopped at the edge of the porch. Her arms hugged her shoulders, and she shivered, wishing with all her might to be home again.

"Evie, come back inside."

Father stood in the doorway, but Evie didn't move. She thought about the house with its cracked walls and dusty furniture. The house in New York, not Michigan. The house beside the cemetery that was not Mom's cemetery. She could feel the tears welling up, stinging her eyes in the cold, and she listened to the hollow sound of the wind as it whipped down the mountains. She shook her head, tasting the salt in her mouth.

"Mom," she whispered, *"why couldn't I have gone with you instead?"*

Evie strained to hear a response in the mournful moan of the wind, but there was nothing. She wiped the tears away with her coat sleeve and stood still, waiting for answers she knew would never come.

CHAPTER FOUR

Tomorrow

For the rest of that week Evie waited for Father to get the phone hooked up and the TV turned on, or maybe to unpack something other than their clothes and sheets, but Father went out to the orchard every day as soon as the sun came up, and then he spent almost the whole day outside among the trees.

Back home Evie would have painted or read books or played with her friend Lawrence down the street, but here she stayed in bed until late and sat for long hours beside the kitchen window, fingering the prayer card Maggie had given her and watching for the strange boy to reappear. Sometimes he was already there when she came downstairs, and other times he emerged from the fog like an apparition, but he was always too far back to see clearly. Twice she almost went out to meet him but couldn't gather her courage. It wasn't that she thought he was a ghost, but the sight of him there, sitting among the graves every day, made the hairs on her neck rise.

Tomorrow, she thought. Tomorrow she would find out who he was, but tomorrow was always one day away. Instead she watched Father go out to the orchard each morning, bundled in his winter work clothes. Sometimes he stopped by her bedroom and leaned against the doorframe, peering in as she pretended to sleep.

Finally one morning Father sat on the side of Evie's bed.

"I know you're not sleeping," he said. "Why don't you come outside with me? You can't stay in here forever, you know."

Evie pulled the old patchwork quilt Gram had made over her head. "It's too cold," she said, her voice muffled. Father peeled the cover away.

"Nah. You can bundle up. It'll be fun. Just you and me exploring the orchard. Beaumont is the perfect place for an adventure."

Evie yanked the quilt back again but only managed to pull it up to her chin. An adventure with Father meant a long walk with lectures about trees and birds and identifying plants.

"Beaumont's just a rotten old town with a lot of dead trees."

"Well, don't you want to help make the trees better? I could sure use an extra set of hands out there."

"They won't get better. They're *dead*."

Father sighed and stroked her hair. "Aww, Evie. We don't know that for sure. Maybe something magical will happen."

"I don't believe in magic anymore," Evie muttered, turning onto her side.

"How about hard work?" Father asked. "Do you believe in that?"

Mom would have raised an eyebrow and said something to make her laugh.

"Yes, the trees are dead, but only because a wicked sorcerer cursed the town, and if you get your lazy butt out of bed, that will break the curse."

Father just sighed. "All right, but soon we start lessons, so there won't be any more sleeping all day. Understand? Maybe I can take you to the library like Maggie suggested. That would get you out of the house."

Evie didn't answer.

"Fine." Father stood up and the bed creaked. "Think it over. In the meantime, you know where to find me."

Evie heard his footsteps as he left the room then disappeared down the hallway. She didn't move until the front door slammed shut below, then she peeked out the corner of her window until she saw Father making his way into the trees.

She listened to the whoosh of the wind, and the tall old willow tree beside her bed *tap, tap, tap*ping against the glass. In the half-light of morning her bedroom looked strange and shadowy. There'd been five bedrooms to choose from, but she and Father had chosen the smallest two, side by side on the orchard half of the house. Evie had chosen hers because there was a painting on the wall of a girl standing in a beautiful garden. The girl's eyes were sad and lost, and Evie wanted to keep her company. She thought how she might have painted the picture differently, but then she shook her head.

There was no more painting without Mom.

Evie sighed. She got up and pulled on her oldest jeans and the flannel shirt she wore on the coldest days back home, then she made her way down the wide staircase to the kitchen. As usual Father had left her an oatmeal packet in a bowl beside the stove. They'd been eating oatmeal, brown bananas, and peanut butter sandwiches left from the trip for over a week because Father hadn't gotten any groceries yet. That was just like him, to take care of the orchard before he even bought butter and eggs.

She pushed the bowl away, and that's when she saw the boy again in the distance, leaning against a gravestone. Evie walked to the kitchen window and pressed her nose against it. Her breath made a foggy circle on the glass. The boy turned, and for a moment it looked as if he'd seen her. She jumped back and wiped the circle away with her sleeve.

She wondered what Mom would have thought of this strange boy, but she knew without a doubt that her mother would have introduced herself by now.

"Hello there. I'm Tally, and you must be the neighborhood ghost."

Then if the boy was alive, he would laugh, and if he wasn't, Mom would find out all his secrets.

Evie chipped small flakes of paint off the window frame. Of course he was alive. He had to be. But why did he sit in the cemetery all day despite the cold? And why did he look so pale? Why had it seemed as if no one at the funeral had seen him?

Tomorrow, Evie thought. *I'll find out he's just a normal boy and that will be the end of it.* Except Father had said there would be lessons soon, and now when she looked out the window she was almost certain the boy was looking toward the house, as if he wanted her to come out.

Evie took a step. Then another. She told herself she was only going to the porch to take a closer look, but she put on her heavy boots and zipped up her thickest coat, as if she were going on a very long trip.

CHAPTER FIVE

Alex

vie walked to the edge of the cemetery, but then she stopped, urging herself to step inside. *It's not any different than visiting Mom,* she thought, but it did seem different. There was something deader than dead about this place. Only how could a cemetery be deader than it already was?

She looked around. There were no flowers or wreaths. No photos or mementos stuck into the dirt. After Mom died they'd taken art supplies and lilies for her birthday, and Evie had buried her favorite glass unicorn beside her mother's grave, but here there was nothing. Just row after row of empty stones with names and dates etched on them. Maybe, like Maggie had said, the people in Beaumont didn't like to remember the dead. Evie imagined putting something new or alive on each stone—but what would the people have liked? And where could she find anything living?

Then she spotted the boy in the distance, his shadowy form appearing out of nowhere. Where had he come from? She waved awkwardly, and the boy stared back at her. Then he started forward, and Evie's pulse raced.

At first she couldn't make out his features, but as he got closer her heart began to pound. His hair was rumpled and dark, and his eyes were a deep brown, just like the boy on the prayer card. He walked all the way to the edge of the cemetery and stopped on the opposite side of the first row of gravestones.

"Hello?" he said.

"Hi," Evie said back, her voice catching in her throat.

The boy leaned forward. "You can see me?"

Evie took a deep breath, then forced it out again. *He wasn't dead. No matter how things might seem.* "Of course," she said. "You're right there."

The boy looked at himself. "I guess I am," he said with surprise, "but I didn't think anyone was going to see me ever again. It's a good thing you came along." He seemed quite satisfied. "I'm Alex. Who are you?"

Evie knew she was staring, so she forced herself to look away. "Evie Adler. My father and I just moved into that old house."

"I used to live past those trees," Alex said, pointing in the distance. "But I guess you could say I live here now."

"Where?"

"The cemetery."

Evie scowled. "You can't live in a cemetery," she said, but Alex crossed his arms over his chest.

"Yes, you can. Look at all these people."

"These people are *dead*."

"Exactly."

"So I'm supposed to believe that you're…"

"I died a week ago." He gave a nod, as if everything were decided. Evie wondered what kind of boy would make up such an elaborate story when he'd just met someone. Except he did look remarkably like the boy on the prayer card. In fact, he looked *exactly* like the boy on the prayer card.

"If you were really dead, you wouldn't be standing here talking to me."

"Oh really?" Alex asked crossly. "What do you know about it?"

Evie almost blurted out that her mom was dead, but she bit her tongue.

"I know what's possible and what's not possible," she said instead. "My father says there's a scientific explanation for everything, so long as one digs deep enough."

"Maybe there *is* a scientific explanation, and maybe it's that I'm dead!"

Alex hopped onto the gravestone nearest to Evie and swung his legs back and forth. "You ought to believe me," he told her. "Ask anyone and they'll tell you what happened. First I was sick in the hospital for a long time, and then I got so sick the doctors said I might as well go home because there was nothing they could do for me. Then my parents took me back to our house and I lay in bed staring at nothing, really, just staring, and that's when I died and everyone was wailing and crying because they said I was gone, but I didn't want to be gone, so I decided I *wouldn't* be."

He said it as stubborn as anyone had ever said anything, and Evie thought of her mom. She'd been sick for a long time, too. At first she'd been able to stay home, but when the cancer got worse she'd lain in the hospital bed just like Alex described, staring at things that Evie couldn't see. Except when Mom died, she really had been gone.

"That's impossible," Evie said. "No one wants to die, but everyone does it anyway. How could you stay behind?"

"I don't know," said Alex, shrugging. "I just stayed,

and now no one can see me but you. And *you* don't even believe me." He leaned forward. "Or maybe you're just too chicken to come over here and see the proof."

"I'm not chicken," Evie said, but her throat clenched as she looked at the graveyard. Alex made clucking noises from his perch on the gravestone.

"What's there to be afraid of?" he asked.

"Nothing," Evie said, hoping she sounded braver than she felt. "I just don't believe you, that's all. Besides," she added, "there's only one graveyard I'll visit and that one's back in Michigan, where my mom is buried."

Alex's expression changed. "Your mom died?"

"From cancer," Evie said, before Alex could ask. "That's what I died from."

Alex hopped down from the stone. "Hey," he said. "Look here. There's really nothing to be scared of." He stepped across the imaginary boundary line that marked the start of the graveyard. "It's only one more step from where you're standing. What difference could one more step make?"

Evie looked down. It was true that one more step would take her into the cemetery, but her feet wouldn't budge.

"We could play games," Alex said. "Soccer and tag and hurdles, like they have at the high school track meets. I'm great at games…"

Evie shook her head.

"I can't," she said. "Father's waiting for me in the orchard."

Alex's face fell. "Wait!" he said. "You're the only one who can see me, so you *have* to stay." He reached out to pull her forward, and his touch was cold as ice. Evie yanked her hand away quick.

"No," she said, more sharply than she'd intended. "It's too cold to stay out here all day."

Alex's brow furrowed defiantly. "You won't believe me, will you?"

All Evie could think about was how solid his hand had felt. She shook her head. "Sorry," she said, but Alex had already turned away.

"Whatever," he muttered.

Evie watched as he walked back across the graveyard and wondered if she'd feel cold and rational like this forever. She couldn't help thinking that when Mom was alive things would have been different.

Once upon a time she would have believed him no matter what.

CHAPTER SIX

Ghosts

ghost couldn't have solid, touchable hands. That was fact, and facts couldn't be argued with. If she told Father about Alex, that would be exactly what he'd tell her. Father would listen carefully, then he'd ask lots of questions, like exactly *how* cold had the hands been, and did the boy have any motivation to lie. Maybe this boy was very sick, Father would say, and he imagines himself about to die. *"There's almost always some truth in every story,"* he'd remind her.

But she couldn't help thinking of what Mom used to say: Sometimes the story is true.

Which was right?

Evie stomped around the perimeter of the house into the orchard. Now that she'd told Alex Father was waiting, she *had* to go see him. She hugged her arms tight around herself as the wind stung her cheeks. Her ears were red with cold and her lips were chapped. It was as if all the warmth of late fall had leaked away through an open window no one knew about.

She found Father exactly as she expected, standing next to one of the trees, holding his pocketknife and a small branch that he'd severed from a limb. He had worry lines across his forehead. Evie had seen Father look like this a thousand times before, and the familiarity brought a spot of warmth inside her chest that even the Beaumont cold couldn't touch.

She waited for him to see her, but it was a long while before he looked up.

"Sprout," he said, finally tearing his gaze from the branch. "You made it outside."

Evie shrugged like it was no big deal.

"What's wrong with the trees?" she asked.

Father frowned. "Black rot, I guess," he said. "Although it doesn't usually look like this." He held out the branch so Evie could see. "Outside the branches are black and gnarled, like something might look after a fire, but inside they're bright green, the way any living thing would be." He paused. "If this really is black rot, it's by far the worst case I've ever seen."

"Is it because of the cold?" Evie asked.

Father shook his head again. "Nah," he said. "Although the ground is nearly frozen solid and it shouldn't be when it's only October. It's more than that. I've been out here every day and haven't seen a single living thing. It's as if…"

Evie knew what he'd been about to say, and her muscles tightened. It was as if everyone was right and there *was* a curse. Something keeping things from growing, keeping it cold and frozen all year long.

Father stopped. "Did you need something?"

Evie knew she shouldn't ask, but she couldn't help herself.

"Do you believe in ghosts?"

Father snorted. "Now you know better than that," he said. "If ghosts were real, they'd be all over the place. There's not a single shred of evidence to suggest they exist. You want to know what ghosts are? They're wishful thinking. People want to believe in them, so they convince themselves that's what they see." He paused, studying her with sharp eyes. "You aren't afraid of that cemetery, are you?"

"No," Evie mumbled.

"Then what made you ask?"

Evie shrugged, and Father's eyes narrowed but he didn't say anything else. Mom would never have given up so easily.

"Arrr! I'll make you walk the plank unless you tell me everything, girlie!"

Father just changed the subject.

"I've decided to go into town to run some errands. I might ask around about what kind of odd jobs I could pick up for the winter to earn some extra money. Maybe I'll stop in later to see Maggie as well. I'd like to find out who owned the orchard before Rodney and when there was last a profitable crop. You want to come?"

Evie shook her head.

There was only one place she wanted to go, but it wasn't in Beaumont. In fact, it wasn't anyplace anymore. After talking to Father she knew the truth.

Home was a ghost.

CHAPTER SEVEN

Mysteries

ater that afternoon Evie stood in her bedroom, staring at the boxes piled on her bed. She was
supposed to be unpacking, but so far she'd only
taken out a few of her and Mom's favorite books.
Peter Pan lay on the top of the stack, and Evie couldn't
help thinking of Alex, wishing he would fly through
her window and take her away to Neverland.

Then she frowned. She was too old for make-
believe now, and Alex was nothing like Peter Pan. He
was an annoying boy who insisted on telling stories
for no good reason when they'd hardly even met.
She forced her attention back to the boxes.

Unpacking—now *that* was real. She'd managed to
empty the kitchen, living room, and bathroom boxes,
but her room was still full of things that needed a
home.

Evie took out her favorite photo of her and Mom,
in their matching Halloween costumes, and wondered

49

where she could hang it. Wouldn't it look odd beside the painting of the girl in the garden? Where would she put the miniature teapot Mom had made her when she was five? Or the easel she'd gotten last Christmas? Or the cookie jar Gram had filled with Evie's favorite homemade peanut butter cups as her going-away present?

She thought about making room on a shelf for the stack of books but wasn't sure where she'd put the dusty old books that were already there. Finally she gave up and sat down beside one of the boxes. She reached in and pulled out the sweater that was folded in the bottom.

Mom's jasmine scent still lingered.

Evie put the sweater on and breathed deep.

Did Alex's parents miss him as much as she missed her mom? Maybe she should go over to his house and tell them that she'd seen him.

Evie frowned. *He's not dead,* she reminded herself. *I touched his hand…*

Except he'd certainly looked dead. He was almost as pale as her mom had been when she died, and when Mom died Evie had been able to reach out and take her hand, holding it tight against her cheek until Father made her let go.

Evie swallowed hard.

She hadn't wanted to remember that, but now the memory came rushing back. She could still feel the coldness of her mother's skin, but maybe some part of her mom had been there and Evie just hadn't known it.

"Mom?" she whispered, but there was no answer. *Of course there's no answer.*

Evie got up and stared out her bedroom window, leaning her forehead against the cold glass. For the first time she noticed that the sun had gone down and Father still wasn't home. She sighed and went downstairs to turn on the porch lights, but that's when she heard noises from outside.

It was so unlike Father to make a racket that she felt her skin prickle, as if a whole pack of ghosts had risen up and were stomping along outside her front door. Then she realized it was only two sets of voices and feet, and the rest of the thumping sounded like bags or boxes being dropped or moved about.

Evie darted to the door and pulled it open to find Father and Maggie standing there with arms full of grocery bags. Father had the house key in one hand and a jug of milk dangling off his ring finger. The wind whistled loudly, and the ends of the bags whipped and pulled.

"Evie," he said, "Maggie's come over for an early

dinner. Sorry it took me so long to run my errands. I got a lead on some jobs in DuPont…Can you grab that?"

Evie's mouth dropped open in surprise, but she managed to catch the milk jug just before it fell.

"Here, grab this, too." Father handed her another bag as he and Maggie hurried inside. Evie had to balance both items on her hip in order to pull the door shut hard against the wind. The loud howl stopped abruptly with a snap as the door latched shut, but a circle of cold lingered.

Father flicked every switch he went past and the house sprang to life, warm and safe. Part of the warmth was Maggie. She stopped in front of the portrait and chucked Rodney on the chin, pausing a moment to smile wistfully, and then she bustled into the kitchen as if she knew exactly where everything was. Which of course she *did*. She went straight to the refrigerator and started unloading eggs and cheese and sticks of butter. Then she opened the top two cupboards and stacked up cracker boxes and instant rice and cans of soup.

"I was over here every day before Rodney died," Maggie said, nodding at Evie's questioning gaze, "but I only lived in this house when I was a child. My father would have sold it years ago if Rodney hadn't insisted on keeping it." She paused, looking around. "I never minded it so much myself. My brother wasn't much of a housekeeper, but I always thought this old house had charm. Now your father tells me he has great plans, starting with whipping up a hot meal for an old woman."

Maggie winked.

"Father invited you?" Evie asked, trying to keep the surprise out of her voice. Maggie laughed and the sound filled the kitchen.

"I think it's safe to say I invited myself, but I didn't have to twist his arm *too* much. I'd been hoping for an invite for a while now, but I wanted to give you time to settle in."

Father chuckled, grabbing the milk and the grocery bag from Evie and setting them on the counter. "I'll start the fire," he said. "We can eat in the living room."

He disappeared across the hall and left Evie standing in the doorway of the kitchen. She crossed her arms over her chest. Then she uncrossed them and kicked at the threshold, but the kitchen looked so bright and inviting with Maggie working away that at last she stepped through.

"So how old are you?" Maggie asked cheerfully, looking Evie over from head to toe. "I'd guess eleven."

Evie frowned. "In two days I will be," she said. She'd almost forgotten about that. "Most people think I'm twelve because I'm tall for my age, but Father says I'll grow into it and be elegant and graceful like my mom, but I don't know…" Evie stopped. It was hard to imagine being graceful when nothing about her seemed to fit.

"Your father told me about your mom on the ride here," Maggie said. "I'm very sorry to hear she passed away."

Evie shrugged and Maggie raised an eyebrow. Evie wondered if Maggie might say something else, but she didn't.

"Eleven is a good age," she said instead, turning the conversation back to Evie's birthday. "I remember turning eleven, although that was a looong time ago."

"How old are you now?" Evie asked, but then she regretted it. No one ever asked adults how old they were. Maggie just laughed.

"Seventy-five," she said, and Evie's eyes went wide.

"That's right. I've lived a long time already. Long enough to see a few things, that's for sure."

Evie waited for more, but Maggie didn't say anything else. Father came back in with his shirt covered in bits of bark and ash from the fireplace, and Evie turned to him instead.

"What are you making for dinner?" she asked.

The ends of his mouth turned up slightly and his eyes sparkled, the way they had back when Evie was small and they'd roasted marshmallows in front of the campfire and played tag in Farmer Dolan's orchard until the sky got too dark to see. It had been a long time since Evie had seen Father's twinkly eyes.

Father swatted at her with the kitchen towel. "Just wait and see," he said. "Probably some gruel, or maybe a bit of hard bread and moldy cheese. Why don't the two of you wait in the living room?"

Maggie looked up and shook herself as if from a dream.

"Perfect," she said. "I have something to give Eve anyways. Isn't that right, Eve?"

She made an exaggerated wink, and Father scratched his beard, his brow furrowing. Evie didn't know if that was right at all, but Father nodded.

"Well, go on then," he said. "Takes time to boil thin broth."

Evie caught herself before her mouth could turn into a smile. She realized what she'd almost done and looked around quickly, as if something bad might happen, but nothing did. They just went into the living room, where Maggie slipped off her shoes and stretched her feet in front of the fire. The rest of the house was cold and drafty, but the fire roared and crackled.

"You must be wondering what I have to give you," Maggie said, and Evie started. She hadn't believed there'd really been something. It was just a game, wasn't it?

Maggie reached into her pocket and took out a box. It was made of stone, and it looked quite heavy but was small enough to fit in the palm of her hand. The lid was held fast with thick twine that was wrapped around it again and again. Evie had never seen anything like it. What kind of present could possibly fit into such a small space? Earrings, maybe, but Evie didn't have pierced ears.

"Take it," Maggie said, handing her the box. "It isn't from me, and no, I don't know what's inside. It was very tempting, but I never looked, because Rodney asked me not to. He was very adamant that you be the one to open it. He said, 'This is for Eve, whenever she may come.' It's a birthday present, I suppose, although how my brother knew it would be your birthday I cannot guess."

Maggie paused, and Evie could tell she was thinking hard.

"The odd thing is," she said, "we once had a sister named Eve. She disappeared just after I was born. I assumed he meant the gift was for her. Rodney never stopped waiting for Eve to come back, and the older he got the more he would talk about the past, telling and retelling that old story of her disappearance. I got tired of it sometimes, if you want to know the truth."

Maggie's eyes were far away.

"I'd forgotten about the box entirely, but last night as I was standing by my dresser, my window latch broke and a gust of wind blew everything onto the floor. I was straightening up when I saw the box, even though I'm certain I had put it in my jewelry case for safekeeping. That's when I wondered if perhaps this wasn't meant to be yours."

"But how would Rodney even know about me?" Evie asked.

Maggie paused, watching the fire.

"Good question," she said. "I suppose your father mentioned you when they spoke on the phone, like he said."

She stopped, as if turning the thought over in her mind.

"Rodney insisted on selling this house to your dad. He told me it was so that I would have the money from the sale, but he sold it for a pittance. Not that I cared. I haven't got any children, and I've got everything I need with the store and my own little apartment above it, but still…Why sell this place? He would have had to move in with me if he hadn't passed away, and Rodney would have *hated* that. He was a private man and my apartment is very small."

Maggie leaned in.

"I'll tell you the truth, Eve," she said. "I thought your dad was just like my brother—a tough, weathered old bachelor come to live out his days alone. Even when I met him to finalize the sale of this house, I thought I was right. But then when he showed up with you, and you have the same name as my long-lost sister! Well…strange, isn't it?"

Maggie's eyes were watching Evie the way a wise old owl watches the world below its treetop. Steady and sharp, taking in every movement.

Evie turned the box over in her hands. "Why would he leave me a present?" she asked out loud, just as Father came in carrying trays full with steaming bowls of soup and crusty bread with honey.

"Who left you a present?" Father asked, setting

the trays down on the small table in front of the fire-place. Evie looked at Maggie, wondering if she should tell, but Maggie nodded.

"Rodney did," Evie said, holding up the box so Father could see. He sat down on the floor between Maggie and Evie.

"Well, open it."

"I can't get the string off," Evie said, trying to force it with her fingers. Father took out his pocket-knife and worked at the thick cords.

"Someone sure wanted this little box to stay shut," he said, struggling to cut through the twine. When the last cord snapped he handed the box back to Evie. Maggie sat up straight and leaned forward, and Evie found herself holding her breath, even though that was silly. What did she expect to find? Still, she slid the lid off quickly.

She didn't expect what was inside.

A single seed.

Evie studied the seed in the flickering firelight, and she thought she felt the brush of a breeze, but then it passed and the fire crackled loudly.

"Well, I'll be…" Maggie's face was suddenly the color of ash.

Father leaned over and plucked the seed from inside the box. He held it between two thick fingers.

"I've never seen a seed that looks like this before," he said. "It seems to be quite old, which is a shame, because I'd love to know what would have grown from it." He frowned. "Must be a symbolic gift, wishing us success with the orchard."

Maggie didn't say anything, just leaned back in her chair, staring at the fire, and Evie had the distinct impression she wasn't telling them something. Father handed the seed back to Evie, and she turned it over on her palm. It made her uneasy, as if she held something alive, and she shivered despite the heat from the fire.

She put the seed back in the box and shut the lid tight. For a moment she couldn't shake the feeling that things were about to change.

Then Father's voice broke the spell.

"Soup's up," he said, reaching for the bowls and passing them to Evie and Maggie. Evie shook herself and turned her attention to the smell of the warm meal. It was a creamy chicken and rice soup—she'd seen the grocery store cans—but Father had added things to it, like he used to do back when he'd cooked for fun. There were carrots, celery, a little bit of corn, and sliced mushrooms. It was quiet while everyone ate, then Evie turned to Maggie.

"So what happened to your sister?" she asked.

Maggie clutched the side of her chair. "Now *that's* a story," she said. "Are you certain you want to hear it?"

Father nodded, but Maggie was looking straight at Evie.

Slowly, Evie nodded, too.

Maggie took a deep breath. "Then I shall start at the beginning…"

CHAPTER EIGHT

Maggie's Story

odney used to say that before Eve disappeared my family was happier than anyone had a right to be. Papa was a botanist and a treasure hunter who traveled all over the world collecting exotic plants and all kinds of artifacts, and Mama stayed home with Rodney and Eve because that's what women did in those days. Papa bought the orchard as a gift so Mama would have a beautiful place to raise their children."

Maggie glanced around the old house as if some shade of her family's happiness might still be found there, but then she shuddered.

"Hard to believe things could change so quickly."

"What went wrong?" Evie asked.

"Well," Maggie answered, "it started with a promise that my father broke. When Mama found out she was pregnant with me, she made Papa promise he wouldn't leave on any of his far-flung trips, and Papa agreed, but not very long afterward he got a phone call from an old friend. As soon as Papa got that call, he packed his bags and took off, and there was nothing Rodney or Mama or Eve could say to change his mind."

"He left?" Evie said, her face growing hot. "After he promised he wouldn't?"

Maggie chuckled. "That's exactly how Eve reacted. And I won't say she was wrong, but when Papa's friend called and said that two archaeologists claimed to have found the original site of the Garden of Eden, Papa couldn't resist."

Evie's eyes widened with excitement. "Mom used to tell me stories about the Garden of Eden!" she said. "Was that really what they'd found?"

"No one can say for certain," Maggie said. "I know Papa believed them…"

"Was there any evidence to support their claim?" Father asked. "Sounds a bit far-fetched to me."

Maggie shrugged. "Well, there were signs of four dried-up rivers that matched those mentioned in the story, and the archaeologists had done quite a bit of research to find the place, but most important, they found a tomb inscribed with an old legend. It didn't date back to the original garden, of course, but it was built many years later by a people who believed the site marked Earth's lost paradise. The tomb held some…relics…that Papa brought back with him, and they were by far his greatest find."

Evie shook her head. "He still should have stayed home."

"Yes," said Maggie solemnly. "You are very much correct. That was the year Rodney turned fifteen and Eve turned eleven. And Mama…well, she died."

Evie drew in a sharp breath.

"I'm afraid it's true," Maggie said, sighing deeply. "She died giving birth to me. I was born earlier than the doctors expected, and Papa didn't make it home in time to be with her."

Maggie studied Evie carefully.

"I'm sorry I never got to know my mother," she said, "but I've had a happy life despite everything. Papa was softer and kinder with me than he'd been with Rodney and Eve…I believe Mama's death taught him things he never would have learned otherwise. Someday I expect to meet my mother in the afterlife so she can see how her baby girl turned out. Won't that be exciting?"

Maggie's eyes twinkled, but Evie bit her lip.

"What happened to Eve?" she asked.

Maggie sighed again. "Rodney said she never forgave Papa, and I suppose that's why she ran away."

"They never found her?"

"No."

For a long time everyone was silent, then Father glanced out the window. "When did the trees stop bearing fruit?"

"Not long after Eve disappeared. Papa didn't take care of them and they withered away."

Evie knew what Father was thinking. Not caring for trees wouldn't cause them to shrivel up into blackened scarecrows, but Maggie didn't pause.

"You can imagine what kind of stir Eve's disappearance caused," she said. "There were more than enough stories about my family to begin with, but when the trees died…that's when the rumor mill really geared up.

"We stayed in this old house for years hoping for Eve's return, but eventually Papa couldn't stand it any longer. He wanted to sell the place, but by that time Rodney was an adult and insisted on taking over, so Papa bought the store in town and we shared the apartment above it while Rodney stayed here."

"Did you mind having to leave?" Evie asked, but Maggie shook her head.

"No. It's difficult to live with tragedy hanging over your head. People lurked around the property, and children dared each other to step foot in the orchard. Some folks blamed Papa for everything, saying he'd unearthed a plague in his travels and it took his daughter and killed all his trees. Others said Rodney had killed our sister and buried her in the apple orchard and *that's* why the trees were cursed.

"Rodney worked with me at the store and picked up odd jobs here and there, but his life was never the same. Plus, he never stopped waiting for Eve to come back. He was the last one to see her alive, and he swore he'd be the first to see her return."

Maggie paused.

"I suppose we'll never know the truth of what happened to Eve," she said, but she glanced at Evie's box as she said it, and Evie had that same strange feeling she'd had before, that perhaps Maggie wasn't telling them the whole story.

Father leaned back. "That's quite a tale."

Maggie nodded and the fire cast shadows on her face.

"You'll hear a lot of talk about the curse around here. People blame it for everything from the orchard being dead to losing their house keys. And it does bother me—can't say it doesn't—but Rodney tried just about everything to bring the orchard back to life. He planted new trees again and again, but they never grew…"

Maggie stopped short.

"Dear me!" she said. "That's not what you wanted to hear, now is it?" She looked at Father apologetically. "Honestly, it's been many years since Rodney was fit enough to work in the orchard. I'm sure whatever disease was creeping through those trees is long gone by now."

Then Maggie stood up.

"Why can't I ever stop talking?" she asked, shaking her head. "Here it is growing late…You folks certainly didn't need to hear all these old stories tonight."

Father got to his feet.

"We've worn you out," he said, and truthfully Maggie did look tired. For the first time since they'd met her, Maggie looked old and her eyes had lost their sparkle.

"I wish I could stay longer," she said, but Evie didn't believe her. In fact, something about the way Maggie hurried made her think the old woman was anxious to leave.

Father followed her to the front door.

"Wait!" Evie said, catching up to them. Father

and Maggie turned around, but Evie wasn't sure what it was she'd been going to say.

"Thank you," she said, "for the present."

Maggie nodded slowly.

"I suspect," she said at last, "that your present holds many secrets."

Then Maggie came close and took Evie's hands in her own, holding them tight.

"Careful, Eve," she whispered. *"Careful."*

CHAPTER NINE

Dreaming

hat night Evie dreamed *she* was the Eve who had disappeared, and she was flying to Neverland with Alex, only when she got there, she found a beautiful garden—just like the one her mom used to tell her about. Her mother was waiting in the middle of it, laughing as she made everything grow. She turned as Evie floated toward her.

"See?" Mom said. "I'm right here waiting for you."

Evie ran forward, but as she ran the garden began to shrivel and the beautiful colors burned into black. Branches coiled around her arms and legs, pulling her away just before her fingertips could reach her mother's outstretched arms.

She woke in her own bed, sitting straight up. Evie looked around wildly, but her room was exactly the same as it had been when she went to sleep, except it was morning now. As usual the sky outside her window was a deep, thick gray.

Evie got up and flicked on the light switch, trying to shake away the dream. She went over to her nightstand and picked up the box with the seed, slid the lid off, and waited. She thought she felt a breeze blow through the room, but it was probably just a draft from her window.

"Mom?" she whispered.

She waited, holding her breath and glancing around for a sign, but nothing happened, and Evie's shoulders slumped. She tossed the box onto her bed.

It was only an old seed.

Evie got dressed and walked across the hall to the spare bedroom where she could look down at the cemetery below. She told herself she wasn't looking for Alex, but she couldn't help spotting him. He was standing on top of a thin gravestone, balancing precariously on one foot. His arms were spread wide and he swayed, righted himself, swayed again, then toppled over. He fell hard on his back, and Evie waited for him to get up, but when he didn't, she dashed downstairs. She sprinted out of the house and into the cemetery, where she found Alex lying on the cold, hard ground.

"Are you all right?" Evie asked, kneeling over him. Alex's eyes were closed and his face was the same ghostly white as always. He didn't move a muscle.

"*Oh no,*" Evie murmured, reaching out to touch his face.

That's when Alex sat up and Evie fell backward in surprise. He grinned mischievously. "You can't get hurt if you're already dead, silly," he said.

Evie's eyes popped.

"What were you doing lying there like that?" she demanded. "I thought you were…"

"Dead?"

Evie punched him on the arm.

"I'm going in," she said, standing up and hugging her arms tight around her thin shirt, but Alex stood up, too, and before she knew it, he'd darted in front of her.

"Wait," he said. "Look! You're standing in the graveyard."

Evie paused and glanced around. She *was* in the graveyard.

"And check this out," Alex added, pointing at the stone he'd been balancing on. "This one's mine."

Sure enough it said: ALEX CORDEZ, BELOVED CHILD 1997–2007.

Evie's breath caught in her throat. The prayer card was still in the pocket of her jeans, where she'd stuck it last, and she couldn't help taking it out to look at it.

Alex Cordez.

"What's that?" Alex asked, reaching around to steal the card out of her hands. He grabbed it, running around the gravestone and spinning in a circle before stopping to look at what he'd gotten.

His face changed suddenly. "It's my prayer card," he whispered. "Where did you get this?"

"Maggie gave it to me," Evie said, blushing.

A shadow moved across Alex's features.

"I wish...," he murmured. "I wish you believed me."

For a long time Evie was quiet, but then she nodded.

"I wish I did, too," she said. "I would have, before my mom died. It's just that... she always told me stories and none of them came true."

"What kind of stories?"

Evie shrugged. "Stories about magical places and amazing things that happen to people when they're least expecting it. I remember once she told me that elves really existed, and if I tried hard enough, one day I would see one. I tried *sooo* hard."

"I believe in elves," Alex said.

"Well, you shouldn't, because elves are made-up. So are leprechauns and fairies and trolls and... ghosts."

Alex leaned over his gravestone and dangled his arms.

"Maybe you shouldn't look with your eyes," he said. "That's what my grandma always told me. She said, 'Look with your ears or nose instead.'"

Evie shivered in the cold. "Or maybe *you* should try thinking with your brain. If you did, you wouldn't be falling off gravestones. The shiny ones are too slippery."

Alex stood up straight and puffed out his chest.

"Oh yeah?" He hoisted himself onto his shiny new stone, knees bent, one foot in front of the other.

"Alex, get down," Evie chided, but inch by inch he straightened his legs.

"You're going to fall again and I'm not going to help you this time."

Slowly he stood up.

"I don't think you should…" Evie stopped and watched as he balanced perfectly, arms wide, eyes straight ahead. Then he grinned down at her.

"See?" he said. "I knew I could do it."

But as soon as he said it, he toppled into a heap on the ground.

"Are you all right?" Evie asked.

"You can't get hurt when you're dead."

Evie made a scoffing noise, but she couldn't help

thinking about her dream and the seed sitting in its box on her bed. She studied Alex as he brushed himself off, wondering if he could possibly be telling the truth.

"Alex, I…"

He looked up.

"What is it?"

Evie paused, but then she shook her head and kicked at a gravestone.

"I better go in," she said. "It's really cold out here."

That night when Evie climbed into bed, she took the seed out of its box and held it in her hand. It was warm, and she tried to remember if it had felt exactly the same the first time she'd touched it.

Again she thought she felt a breeze, silky and soft, quiet as a lullaby.

Then, in her mind, the image of a tree sprang so vividly and suddenly to life that Evie dropped the box in surprise. It fell onto the bed and the seed rolled off the side. Evie got down and knelt quickly, catching it just before it rolled between the floorboards.

Strange.

The tree was only in her mind, but Evie hadn't let her imagination run away with her in a long time. *It must be because of Alex,* she thought. Then she thought of something else.

Mom would have liked this.

The idea snuck in before she could stop it.

Evie put the seed back in the box and shut the lid tight. *No more stories.* Tomorrow she would plant the seed and be done with it. She'd give it back to Rodney.

Give it back…

The words echoed in her mind as she shut off the light.

CHAPTER TEN

Birthday Wishes

vie's first thought the next morning was planting the seed.

It was early when she woke, and she dressed hurriedly, then crept down the creaky wooden steps. She was telling herself how relieved she'd be when the seed was gone, when she heard clanging from the kitchen and Father poked his head into the hall.

"Don't think you're sneaking by without eating on your birthday."

Her birthday. She'd forgotten all about it.

Or maybe she hadn't wanted to remember.

Evie stuck the stone box into the pocket of Mom's sweater and went into the kitchen.

"I'm not sneaking by," she said, even though it hadn't been true a moment ago. Still, now that she could smell the bacon and eggs, she was beginning to forget why she'd been in such a hurry. Father pulled plates out of the cupboard and set two homemade biscuits on them. Then he kissed the top of Evie's head and held her closer than he had for a long time.

"Happy birthday." He went back to the stove, and Evie wondered if he was thinking the same thing she was. It was her first birthday without Mom. For once she was glad to be in Beaumont, without friends and family to make a big deal about things.

Father slid the omelet and bacon out of the pan and split them between their two plates, then he cleared his throat. "I've been wanting to talk with you," he said, carrying the plates over to the table so he could sit down across from Evie. There was a long pause, and Evie knew Father was working up his courage.

She picked at her food, and he shifted in his chair.

"I know you didn't want to come here," he said finally. "I'm sure you heard your aunt and uncle whispering about your father going off the deep end, buying up some long-dead orchard that never made any money."

It was true she'd heard the whispering.

"People lose their senses from grief. Poor man."

"Can't someone put a stop to this nonsense?"

"It's just a shame Evie has to suffer for it. What would Tally have said?"

"I tried to explain about buying this place," Father said, buttering his biscuit, "but I don't think I ever did a good job, and now here you are with no one but me to celebrate your birthday with."

He put down his knife. "Darn it, Evie," he said, "I had to buy this orchard. I don't think I ever told you that when Rodney called me, he said he'd gotten my number from Talia Adler."

Evie sat up straight. "Mom knew Rodney? How? Why didn't you tell me before?"

"Because there's nothing to tell," Father said, shaking his head. "Your darn mother always had to be so mysterious about things. I have no idea how she would've met an old hermit in upstate New York or why she would have given him our phone number. Everything always had to be an adventure or…"

Father slammed his fist against the table. The plates clattered loudly and Evie jumped.

"Lord, I wish she were here."

He paused and his jaw clenched tight.

"You know, once everyone started whispering, I wanted to prove them wrong. I wanted to prove I could make things grow, make things…"

He stopped short of saying "live."

"Now I don't know, Evie. I've never seen trees so bad off. I'll have to cut away most all the branches and burn them before spring if there's hope of bringing them back, and even then I'll probably have to plant new trees. Plus, I might need to pick up some odd jobs for extra income to tide us over until the first harvest. That's a lot of work for one man, and it might take several seasons before we have fruit."

Evie studied her breakfast plate.

"I want you to be happy here. It hasn't been easy for either of us since your mom died. Most days I miss her so bad that's all I think about. I want you to know that you can talk to me about anything," Father said. "I've got my work cut out for me here, but you come first."

Evie thought about Alex and the seed, but Father was already turning away, reaching behind him.

"I've got to get back to the orchard," he said, "but I wanted to give you your birthday presents first. You should be getting a package in the mail today from Gram and your aunt and uncle. You can open it when it gets here." He handed her two presents, both wrapped in leftover newspaper. "These are from me. I forgot to pick up wrapping paper," he added apologetically.

Evie opened the first box. Inside were two pairs of jeans that wouldn't bare her ankles to the cold.

Only they weren't the pretty ones Mom would have picked out.

"These ought to fit better," Father said, taking several quick bites of his breakfast. Evie nodded. She took the second present and unwrapped it. This one was smaller and heavier, and when the newspaper came off she was looking at a book with an apple on the cover.

"The lady in the bookstore recommended this one. It's about a girl whose mom gets sick and they have an apple orchard, so I thought maybe…"

Mom would have chosen something about castles or fairies.

Father shifted uncomfortably, and Evie knew she should say thank you, but she couldn't force the words out. Instead Father reached behind him for one last present. He took a single green envelope off a pile of loose papers on the counter.

"This one isn't from me." He took a deep breath. "Your mom asked me to give it to you on your birthday, so…here."

Evie stared at the envelope. Her lips parted and tears welled in her eyes, but Father wiped them off before they could slide down her cheeks.

"No crying on your birthday," he said, nodding at the card. "Save it for after breakfast so it'll last a while." He got up awkwardly, his shoulders tense. "I'll check on you later," Father said. "I've just got to make some progress with the pruning and then…"

Father stopped, studying Evie's face.

"Aww, Evie," he whispered. "It won't feel like this forever. Just wait until spring and things will come alive again. That's why I'm doing all this. You know that, don't you?"

Evie stared at the envelope with her name written in Mom's swirly handwriting.

"Not everything will come alive," she said, and Father frowned.

"No," he said, "not everything, but maybe a few things that haven't felt alive in a long time. Maybe we could hope for that much."

CHAPTER ELEVEN

The Only Gift That Counts

fter breakfast Evie sat alone in the living room with the unopened card from her mother on her lap. The house was dark and chilly, and the sound of Father's chain saw was far away.

"Father always remembers you, even when it seems like he's forgotten."

Evie wondered if that was true.

The package from Gram, Aunt Carol, and Uncle Pete had arrived and their presents lay strewn about the floor—they were practical gifts like new sneakers, a long red scarf Gram had knitted, and a wool sweater from Aunt Carol. Father's book and her new jeans lay on the floor, too, but the only gift that mattered was the card.

Evie pressed the envelope to her cheek, feeling the grain of the paper, then she held it to her nose, hoping it might smell like Mom, but it didn't. The paper was homemade though, and Evie remembered the way her mother used to make paper in her studio, blending up the recycled bits of wrapping paper, cardboard, and old mail with water and starch and then pressing the milky mix onto screens to dry. Sometimes she pressed leaves or pretty beads into the new paper, and Evie wondered if the card inside would have something special on it. Something Mom had made just for Evie.

One last thing…

It was too bitter to be sweet. Once she read the words, there would be nothing new ever again. *I don't want a card,* she thought. *I want Mom back.* But that was one birthday gift she knew she wouldn't get.

Evie set the card on the mantel so that it was just peaking out from behind the candlesticks, and reached into her pocket for the stone box instead.

Slowly, carefully, she lifted the lid to see the seed inside. Again she felt a breeze and thought of a tree—not one kind of tree, but a tree that seemed to be every kind at once—its branches spread wide against the sky.

She wasn't frightened this time though, so she let the image fill her mind. She imagined the tree growing taller and stronger, and around its base plants of all kinds bloomed in abundance. Evie could almost smell the earthy scent of rich soil and fragrant flowers, and when she closed her eyes she imagined sun on her face.

Then she shut the lid abruptly, squeezing it shut until her fingers hurt. Why had she let herself imagine that again?

She wished she could tell Mom about the seed. She stared at the barely visible edge of the card and knew she ought to open it and see what was inside, but her fists clenched tight. What good were words on a page? You couldn't tell a card your secrets.

Evie slipped the box back into her pocket.

Father said I could talk to him about anything, she thought, and Father was still here. He could listen and respond and maybe he'd even hold her tight the way he used to when she was small.

Evie grabbed her coat and her new scarf, and headed outside. The front door snapped shut behind her, and she made her way to the orchard, where she found Father working a couple rows in, taking down small twisted branches. He wore his safety glasses and his thick winter hat with the earflaps, so he didn't notice Evie until she was right beside him.

"Sprout," he said, his cheeks flushed from the

cold. "You snuck up on me." He set down his chain saw.

Evie only nodded and slipped the box with the seed out of her pocket.

"I…I wanted to show this to you."

She slid the cover off without saying a word and handed it to Father. Now that he wasn't sawing, the orchard was silent and still. Evie waited for the wind to pick up or for warm sunshine to bathe Father's face, but nothing happened. She even reached out her finger to touch the surface of the seed, but it was cold.

"I've already seen it," Father said. "This is why you interrupted me?"

Evie stared at the box, willing the seed to do for Father what it had done for her.

"It's just…" She paused. "I wondered if maybe it was special or…"

Father laughed soft and gruff.

"It's just a seed, Sprout," he said. "Why don't you plant it and see if something grows? Start it out in the house, like a science project."

Evie opened her mouth, then shut it again.

"I want to plant it out here," she said. "In the orchard."

Father shrugged. "Well, I'm not so sure it will grow this time of year, but then again I'm not so sure my trees are going to grow, either. Heck, I'd say plant it anywhere you'd like. I bet you'll find the perfect spot."

He handed the box back.

"I'm going to have my chain saw out all afternoon," he added, "so don't be sneaking up on me again."

Evie nodded, but she stood still, hoping Father might reach out and wrap her up in a bear hug, but he just studied her carefully.

"You okay?" he asked. "Was it a good letter from your mom?"

Evie shrugged, still staring at the seed. "I didn't open it yet."

"You want to talk?" Father asked, but she shook her head even though the answer was yes. She *did* want to talk, but not to Father.

She needed to find Alex.

CHAPTER TWELVE

The Search for a Stone

Evie peered into the graveyard.

"Alex?" she called, but there was no answer. She turned to go back inside but caught sight of a piece of black wool sticking out from beneath the billowing robe of a marble angel. The angel stood on a platform and it was as tall as a man with its arms outstretched, its robe making a circle around a smaller statue of a child. Only in this case there were two children, and one of them was Alex.

Evie took a deep breath and crossed the boundary line into the graveyard. She jogged over and knelt down to shake Alex awake. He stared up at her with sleepy eyes.

"Did I doze off?" he asked, and Evie nodded. Alex's hair was mussed and he looked as pale as the marble statue, but he grinned.

"Hey, that's two days in a row," he said, sitting

up. He squeezed out from beneath the angel's robe. "I didn't even have to drag you here today."

Evie narrowed her eyes. "I don't think nearly killing yourself yesterday qualifies as dragging me here," she replied, but Alex just smiled smugly.

"It does if I planned it that way."

"If you planned it," Evie said, "then how did you know I'd be watching right at that exact moment?"

"Ghost powers," Alex said.

"You've got to be kidding. Ghosts do *not* have superpowers."

"How do you know so much about being a ghost? Have *you* ever been one?"

"No," Evie said, "but—"

"Then you don't know."

Evie sighed. "Did anyone ever tell you that you're the most aggravating—"

"You like me," Alex interrupted before she could finish.

"Do not."

"If you didn't, you wouldn't keep coming back. Besides, everybody always loved me. Especially grown-ups. And girls."

Alex wiggled his eyebrows, but Evie rolled her

eyes. "Maybe I just need your ghost powers," she said. "If they're *real,* of course."

"They are," Alex said, straightening. "Just tell me what you want me to do."

"Fly," Evie said.

"I haven't learned that yet."

"Make yourself invisible then."

"I already am."

"Conjure up a magic light or something."

Alex held out his hand, palm up.

"There's nothing there," Evie protested.

"Of course there is! It's not my problem if you can't see it."

Evie blew her bangs out of her eyes with an impatient breath. "Fine. Then how about finding a gravestone?"

"Which one?" Alex asked.

"Rodney Clayton."

Alex's face screwed up in disbelief. "Old Rodney? Why would you want to find *his* grave?"

Evie paused, trying to decide if she should show him the seed. "Can I trust you?" she asked.

"With what?"

"A present. If I show it to you, will you promise not to tell anyone?"

"I'm dead, silly," Alex reminded her. "Who would I tell?"

Evie took the box out of her pocket. "This was a birthday present from Rodney."

Alex leaned forward. "But old Rodney died months ago. When was your birthday?"

"It's today," Evie said. "Rodney left this for me."

Alex shuddered. "I don't know what it is, but I bet it's bad luck. Everyone said old Rodney was cursed."

"Well, I don't believe in curses."

Evie slid off the lid so Alex could see the seed. Despite herself, she held her breath, equally expecting both a gush of wind and nothing at all. She even closed her eyes, shutting them tight against…what?

At first there was nothing. Evie opened her eyes, disappointed. *See? Nothing happened.* Then she noticed Alex, and his eyes were dancing with excitement.

"What is it?" he breathed. "Is it magic?"

"I don't know," Evie said. "It's just a seed…I think." She wasn't sure what she believed anymore. "Did it do something? I mean, did you feel a breeze or sunlight on your face or anything?"

Alex nodded. "It was warm, like springtime."

Evie's chest clenched tight. "Will you help me look for Rodney's grave?" she asked. "I think that's where I should plant it."

She waited for Alex to say yes, but instead he took a step back.

"No. Way."

Evie's jaw dropped. "What? Why not?"

"People in town wouldn't let the old man be buried in the cemetery because they thought he might curse all the dead people. He's buried in the orchard instead. In the exact center."

Evie glanced toward the twisting rows of apple trees waiting like an army of giants standing guard. "So we'll go into the orchard then," she said, but Alex's pale face got even paler.

"No one goes in there," he whispered. "Old Rodney killed his sister in that orchard, and now her ghost sucks all the life out of it. If you step inside the tree line, she'll chop you up with the ax she stole from Simon Mackler's place. It's true, Evie. One day that ax was sitting on his porch, and the next day it was missing."

Evie put both hands on her hips.

"You believe all that?" she asked, and Alex nodded solemnly.

"Well, my father goes into the orchard every day," Evie said, "and he hasn't gotten chopped up yet. Besides," she added, "what could a ghost do to *you*?"

"I bet she could think of something," Alex said.

"Now who's chicken?" Evie asked, but it didn't do any good. Alex only shook his head, and Evie felt her hopes drifting away. She could tell that his mind was made up, and if there was one thing she already knew about Alex, it was that he could outstubborn anyone she'd ever met.

CHAPTER THIRTEEN

Truth and Lies

For the rest of the day Evie thought about the curse. She stared at Rodney's portrait in the hall-way, and his eyes bore into hers as if he was trying to tell her that the stories weren't true. He looked deter-mined, but kind, too, like someone who would've been a good big brother. Maybe that was why he'd given her the seed. To prove that he hadn't killed his sister.

But how could a seed prove anything? Unless it was magic…

Evie thought about what Mom had said about magical stories.

"They're not always kind, Evie. Sometimes there are wolves waiting to eat little children and evil things lurking in the woods. Don't ever wish that life was a fairy tale."

Only now Evie felt as if she were stuck in one.

"Mom," she whispered, "how do I know what's true?"

She wished there was someone besides Father or Alex that she could ask. Someone who might see things like she did. Then she stopped. Actually there *was* someone.

Maggie.

Evie ran down the hallway to where Father had posted a list of emergency numbers. He always included a neighbor, and since they didn't know anyone else in town it would have to be Maggie. She scanned the list.

Grandma, Uncle Pete, Aunt Carol…There it was, written in Father's chicken scratch down at the bottom of the paper. Maggie Clayton: 555-7872.

Evie dialed the phone with unsteady fingers, and it rang twice before someone picked it up.

"This is Clayton's Farm Supplies. How can I help you?"

"Maggie?"

"Yes?"

Evie swallowed hard. She hadn't stopped to think about what she might say.

"It's Evie. Evie Adler."

"Is everything okay? You sound upset."

"I'm fine," Evie said, "but I need to ask you something. About the seed."

There was a long pause—so long that Evie wondered if Maggie had hung up the phone.

"Did you plant it?" Maggie asked at last.

"Not yet," Evie said, "but sometimes it seems... strange... and I thought about planting it in the orchard only... someone said..."

Suddenly Evie wished she'd never picked up the phone, but Maggie just sighed.

"They said it was cursed?"

"Yes," Evie said.

Maggie's voice was soft. "Perhaps we should talk. Can you get your father to bring you to the store? I can't leave right now, but once you're here I could maybe slip away for a few moments."

"Father will never leave work in the middle of the day," Evie said, but Maggie only clucked.

"Have you asked him yet?"

"No."

"Well, why don't you see what he says?"

"All right," Evie said, hoping Maggie was correct.

"I'll be waiting for you."

The phone disconnected with a soft click, and Evie stood still, cradling the receiver. She was sure Father would say no, but she hung up the phone and walked back down the hallway, grabbing her coat, then lingering for a moment on the front porch to study the lines of trees.

Alex was right. They did look cursed.

She swallowed hard, then headed toward the orchard, following the sound of Father's chain saw until she saw him ahead of her, hacking away at branch after branch as if he were battling a huge ogre. She waited a long time, but when he didn't turn around, she finally moved up next to him, then touched his shoulder softly.

Father jumped and shut off the saw abruptly.

"I thought I told you not to sneak up on me again," he growled.

Evie almost turned around, but then she thought about the seed and instead she planted her feet.

"No, you didn't," she said. "You told me I could talk to you about anything, but you lied."

Father opened his mouth, but Evie didn't stop.

"You lied about us moving next to a cemetery; you lied about Mom knowing Rodney; you lied about me coming first. All you want to do is work, even on my birthday. You'd be happier if I wasn't even here."

Father set down the saw and took Evie by both shoulders. "Don't you ever say that," he said, shaking her. "It's not true. I didn't lie about the cemetery or your mom knowing Rodney. I just didn't tell you everything."

Tears sprang to Evie's eyes, but she fought them back. "What's the difference?"

"It's…well…" Father shook his head. There was a long silence, then finally he said, "I guess there isn't much of one." He let go of her shoulders. "I didn't mean to get angry. Just…tell me what you need."

"I want to go into town."

"Right now?"

"Yes. It's my birthday and you've worked the whole day. I want to go see Maggie."

Father glanced at the trees and Evie knew what he would say.

"There's more work than I can handle out here. I can't afford to take a break if we want apples next fall."

She thought about all the times since Mom died that she'd done exactly what he wanted, but this time she wasn't going to take no for an answer.

"It's important," Evie said. Then she fixed him with the same look that Mom had used when she really wanted something—her head cocked to one side and her eyebrows raised in expectation.

Father opened his mouth, then he turned, and

for a moment she thought she saw tears glistening, but then he cleared his throat and nudged the pile of branches with his foot.

"Okay," he said at last. "I suppose that's not too much to ask."

CHAPTER FOURTEEN

The Rest of the Story

On the ride into town Evie couldn't stop fidgeting.

What did Maggie know about the seed?

She was certain there was something Maggie hadn't told her. It felt as if she'd been doing a jigsaw puzzle and the final piece was waiting at Maggie's shop. As soon as the car stopped she jumped out, hoping she could beat Father inside.

"Hold your horses," he said, taking long strides to catch up, but when they got into the store, Maggie was behind the counter helping a customer. Evie stood first on one foot and then on the other, and Maggie nodded when she noticed them.

"Simon," she said to the man at the counter, "this here is Frank Adler and his daughter, Eve. They bought Rodney's place and Frank's going to try and bring back that orchard. It'll be nice to have apples again, wouldn't you say?"

The man at the counter frowned. "Shouldn't be messing with those trees," he grumbled. "You'll make things worse than they already are. Nothing grows in these parts—not even weeds in the lawn—and it's 'cause of them trees sucking all the life out of things. If you ask me, they're trouble. Townsfolk ought to have burned them down years ago whether Rodney liked it or not."

Evie felt Father tense up beside her, but Maggie smacked the man's change down on the counter with a loud thud.

"Well, no one asked you, did they?" she said, before Father could respond. "It's not very neighborly of you to set about complaining before you've even said hello."

The man snorted.

"Didn't intend to be neighborly," he said, stuffing his change into his pants pocket. Then he turned and sidled past Father in a way that made Evie feel like he'd meant there to be a fight. Father's eyes followed him until he disappeared out the door.

Maggie shook her head.

"Don't mind him," she clucked as the front door slammed shut. "Folks are full of ignorance and superstition, but they'll get over it soon enough."

Will they? Evie wondered. *Or are they right?*

Father frowned at the floor.

"I'm going to check out those saw blades in the back," he said, without meeting Maggie's eyes. Evie watched as he turned down one of the aisles, then as soon as he was out of sight, she leaned in.

"Maggie," she whispered, "did Rodney ever say anything about that seed? I mean, before he gave you the box?"

Maggie took a deep breath. She looked as if she was making up her mind about how much to say, but finally she nodded. "Yes," she said. "But his stories didn't make any sense, so I never believed them." She leaned forward. "I must know…Why did you say that the seed seemed strange?"

Evie paused, wondering if Maggie would scoff at her the way Father would.

"I've felt a breeze," she said, "just like the wind that blew everything off your dresser. And it makes me think of a beautiful tree, almost as if it's calling me to plant it."

Maggie's face shifted in surprise. "I see," she said. She paused. "So now you want to know where that seed came from, because you suspect I didn't tell you everything…"

"Yes," Evie said.

Maggie stared out the store window. She looked

as if she was about to say something, then she stopped and started again.

"There *is* more, but it's not a pleasant story. Still, it's natural that you would want to know."

Evie leaned forward. "Please will you tell me?"

"Well...," Maggie said, "it has to do with my sister, Eve. You see, when Papa came home from that trip he brought back three relics, like I told you. What I didn't tell you was that the relics were three seeds that were said to be from the Garden of Eden. The seeds were found in the tomb I told you about—the one inscribed with the legend—and they were said to bring great life to those who needed it most, only they came with a warning."

"What was it?" Evie asked.

"It was cryptic," Maggie said. "Something about life being granted at the cost of life being taken away. It spoke of making choices, if I remember correctly..."

Maggie glanced at Evie's wide eyes.

"Of course, that could mean anything. And honestly I don't think those seeds are *really* from the Garden of Eden. Nor do I think they hold any sort of power," she said, straightening. "Papa couldn't have truly believed in them either or else he would have kept them locked up, and Eve never could have stolen them."

Evie's breath caught.

"Oh yes," Maggie said. "Eve stole them out of spite and took them to the orchard to plant them. Rodney chased her, trying to get them back, but she wouldn't stop. He lost sight of her for only a moment, but it was long enough. When he found her again she had already planted the first seed.

"I remember him telling me about the look on her face...how she stared upward as if she were seeing something very beautiful, only Rodney saw nothing. Then she walked forward, and he called to her, but in a blink she had disappeared and no one has seen her since. All that was left were the remaining two seeds in their boxes."

Maggie sighed.

"Rodney believed those seeds led someplace magical—he'd ramble on and on about all the possibilities, convinced that the orchard had paid the price for Eve's choice, but I've never been able to accept that. I know for a fact that Rodney planted the remaining seeds again and again because I caught him several times, but obviously nothing happened. Papa and I would find the holes where he'd buried them, then dug them up again. I think even Papa planted them a few times." She paused. "I was sure they were long gone."

Evie was quiet, trying to imagine Rodney as a fifteen-year-old boy watching his sister disappear and trying desperately to find her again.

"The seed must have taken Eve to the Garden of Eden," Evie said, but Maggie shook her head.

"Impossible. The stories about Eden are clear— no one is allowed back into paradise. It's said to be guarded by cherubim and seraphim with flaming swords."

Evie paused, her breath quickening.

"What about a different sort of garden then?"

"Maybe someday we'll each find our own perfect garden instead."

"I suppose," Maggie said, but she didn't look at all certain.

Evie could barely force the next words out of her mouth. "So is my seed one of the ones from your father's trip?"

Maggie drummed her fingers on the counter, then glanced toward the back of the store, where Father was shopping.

"I can't say for certain," she said, sighing, "but knowing Rodney, I'd guess the answer is yes. But on my word, Eve, I still don't think that seed took my sister anywhere."

Evie's eyes popped. "Where else could she have gone?"

"She could have run away like everyone said. People don't simply vanish. Maybe Rodney only *thought* he saw her disappear, but really she turned a corner and ran because he'd caught her doing something naughty. You know how many twists and turns are in that orchard. Besides," she added, "all you've got to do is look around Beaumont to see that no great life has been imparted here, or anywhere else for that matter."

"But what about *my* seed?" Evie asked, her face flush. "It's not just an ordinary seed. I'm sure of it..."

Evie was rushing so much she didn't notice Father coming up behind her.

"Sure of what?" he asked.

Maggie and Evie exchanged glances, and Evie pleaded with her eyes for Maggie not to tell. Maggie sighed deeply.

"Sure there's going to be snow soon," she said at last, ringing up Father's new saw blade. Evie grinned gratefully, but Maggie stared forward, deep in thought. The fingers of one hand hit the keys on the cash register as her other hand rested on the saw blade. She pulled away quick as a small gash formed on her finger. She wrapped it in her apron but not before a single drop of blood trickled down the blade.

Father reached across the counter to help, but Maggie jumped.

"Should have been paying attention," she muttered. "If I'd been watching what I was doing…" She laughed nervously. "There's nothing to worry about," she said, looking straight at Evie.

Nothing to worry about.

But Maggie's eyes said something different.

Father hoisted the saw blade off the counter, and Evie and Maggie followed him out to the truck.

"Wait," Maggie said, just as they were about to get in. "I forgot your change. Eve, why don't you run in with me and I'll get it for you."

Evie nodded, then she dashed away before Father could protest. When they were inside Maggie scooped Father's change off the counter and folded it into Evie's palm.

"Now I'm not saying I believe all this nonsense," she said, "but stay away from that seed just in case. Promise you won't plant it."

Evie paused.

"Will you find a beautiful garden, Mom?"

"I hope so, Evie."

"Then I will meet you there."

She shoved Father's change in her pocket and crossed her fingers tight.

"I promise," she said, but she didn't mean it.

CHAPTER FIFTEEN

One Giant Step

When Evie and Father got back home, it was too dark to go outside. Evie thought about sneaking out to the orchard right then, but the idea of being out there in the pitch black by herself sent chills down her spine.

Instead she lay in bed awake most of the night, tingling with the possibility that Mom was waiting for her in a beautiful garden, just like she'd said. She remembered the way she used to imagine her own garden—full of waterfalls and rainbows and animals of every sort.

"No vegetables?" Mom asked, curling beside Evie on her bed.

"Not a single one," Evie answered.

Mom laughed. "I'd have vegetables in my garden. Plus, there would be an orchard just like the one Father works in, and a little house just like our house, and a little girl just like—"

"Hey, that's not a garden!"

"Oh, but it is," Mom said. *"The world would be my garden, Evie, my love. The whole entire world."*

Evie drifted off to sleep imagining her mother's arms circling around her. When she woke, she could almost feel the warmth of her mom's form snuggled next to her. She reached out to the space where her mother would have been, only it was empty.

For a long time Evie lay still, waiting for the ache to subside. Then she spotted the box on her nightstand and ran her finger over its smooth surface.

"Will you take me to my mom?" she whispered.

From the corner of her eye she saw that her clock read ten A.M. She must have been dreaming all morning. Slowly Evie got out of bed and pulled on her clothes and shoes, then she washed her face and ran downstairs to the kitchen. She looked out the window but didn't see Alex in the graveyard, so she stepped out the front door to find him.

She didn't have to go far. Alex was sitting on the porch, his hair rumpled and his arms crossed.

"Finally," he said. "I've been waiting all morning."

"I was just going to look for you," Evie said.

"That's because I called you with my ghost powers." Alex stood up. "Did you plant the seed yet?"

"No, but you'll never guess what I found out about it."

"You found out you could plant it somewhere other than the orchard?" Alex asked, but Evie only sighed.

"Stop being such a fraidycat. I talked to Maggie and it turns out the seed Rodney gave me came from the Garden of Eden!"

Alex narrowed his eyes. "Are you making this up?"

"It's true," Evie said, crossing her heart and spitting on the ground. "There were three of them, and Maggie's sister planted the first one just before she disappeared. Rodney believed it took her away to someplace magical, and he *must* have been right." She paused, leaning in. "Think about it, Alex. My mom said everyone has a beautiful garden waiting just for them, only we can't find them until after we die. But maybe…"

"Who would want to find a pile of old vegetables after they die?"

Evie threw up her hands in exasperation. "It wouldn't be a pile of old vegetables. Use your imagination! Everyone's garden would be just the way they'd want it to be. There could be streams or mountains or white clouds…"

"Sounds like heaven," Alex said, but then he

frowned. "I thought your mother's stories didn't come true."

"This one is different," Evie said. "The seed isn't something Mom made up. Maggie's father found it on a real expedition, and it'll be such an adventure when I plant it…"

Alex chipped at the paint flaking off the porch banister.

"I like adventures," he said. "I always have. I'm the bravest person I know…" He stopped. "At least, most of the time."

Evie hopped off the porch, heading toward the trees, and Alex followed. She counted the rows as she went, then divided by two to mark the center.

"X marks the spot," she said, tying her new red scarf around a low branch. Then she stepped into the orchard. "It's only one more step," she said, turning back to Alex. "What difference could one more step make?"

Alex studied the trees ahead of him.

"Can I see the seed one more time?" he asked.

Evie took the box out of her pocket and slid off the lid. A gust of wind swirled around them, and Alex jumped.

"Don't you want to know if it's magic?" Evie whispered.

Finally Alex closed his eyes and held his breath. Then he took one giant step into the orchard. When he was across, he opened first one eye, then the other, and looked around wildly, but nothing happened.

"See?" Evie said. "That wasn't so bad."

He let out his breath in a loud whoosh.

"I knew it wouldn't be," he said, but his eyes darted anxiously.

Evie stuck out her hand. "No turning back until we've planted the seed on old Rodney's grave," she said. "Deal?"

Alex hesitated, but at last he placed his ice-cold hand on hers.

"No turning back," he said. "Not even if we find a ghost."

CHAPTER SIXTEEN

Signs

he sound of Father's chain saw grew fainter as they walked, and in the back of her mind, Evie knew she and Alex were going farther away from the old house than Father would have allowed, but the trees went on and on, stretching toward the mountains with no end in sight.

At first Alex walked several feet behind her, glancing around nervously, but she felt him drawing closer the farther they walked. Evie kept her eyes on the path ahead, but she couldn't help shivering with excitement when she thought of what might come next.

"Do you think maybe we'll get to heaven through this garden?" Alex asked after a while.

"Maybe," Evie said.

"I'd like to go there," Alex whispered, and Evie shifted.

"What about your family? Don't you want to stay here with them?"

"No," Alex said. "It's not like it was before. We used to do all sorts of fun stuff together—like my dad was teaching me to ski and my mom and I used to play Monopoly every day after school—but now they don't even see me. It isn't fair."

"I know," Evie said. And she did know. It *wasn't* fair. But maybe Rodney's gift would make things better.

"Alex," she asked, her feet crunching against the brittle grass, "what were you like when you were alive?"

"Perfect. Just like now."

Evie rolled her eyes. "For real."

This time Alex thought it over.

"I could make anyone laugh, no matter what. And once I won a prize for writing the best story, and it got published in the school paper. Plus, I used to read all the time—even stuff Ma got mad about."

"My mom and I read together every night," Evie said. "Sometimes when she wasn't around, I'd skip ahead to the end of the book, and then I'd pretend to be surprised when we got there."

"Once," Alex said, "I pretended I was lost for an entire day because I got in trouble in school, but really I was upstairs hiding under the bed the whole time."

"What did you do to get in trouble?"

"I brought a whoopee cushion to class and put it on the teacher's chair."

Evie laughed.

"Did it work?"

"No," he said, but he grinned impishly.

Evie tried to remember the last time *she'd* gotten in trouble. It was a strange thing to miss, but it had been a long time since she'd done anything fun that might have gotten her punished.

Finally she thought of something.

"Father and I ate half a batch of cookie dough once. We both got sick and Mom was furious."

"Cookie dough was my favorite food," Alex said. "Other than pizza and fried chicken and tacos and—"

"Hey! It's not a favorite if it's more than one."

Alex laughed, but then he got quiet again.

"How long ago did your mom die?"

"It's been ten months now," Evie said.

"How can you live without her?"

Evie studied the darkened trees. "Sometimes I don't want to."

Alex nodded as if he understood. "I go home at night and sit by my parents even though they can't see me. My mom's so sad she says she wants to die, and I think maybe she will."

"She won't," Evie said. "It just feels that way."

"I try to tell her I'm right here, but she doesn't hear me."

Evie breathed out long and slow. "I wish my mom were here."

"How do you know she's not? Maybe you just don't see her."

"I'll always be with you, no matter what."

Evie shook her head. "I don't think so. I asked her to send me a sign if she was nearby but she never has."

"I've sent people signs," Alex said. "Lots of them, but nobody sees them, either."

"Really?" Evie asked, ducking under a tree branch. "What kind of signs?"

"Signs to tell people good-bye. So they won't feel sad once I'm completely gone. I took out all my most secret stuff from my dresser drawer and brought it to the cemetery—like letters and a journal I wrote in—but my mom won't come out here and my dad won't leave my mom, so no one noticed and I put it all back again. Then I made my mom a present and left it outside her door, but she never saw it."

"What sort of present?"

"A wooden heart that said 'I Love You' in the middle."

Evie's eyes watered. "That's so sad," she said, remembering her mother's card. "But maybe your mom did notice and she was saving it for later."

"Do you think?" Alex asked. Then he shrugged. "It doesn't matter," he said, only he didn't look like he meant it.

They turned a corner and the ground sloped downward, then just as Evie was about to say something, her foot hit a square gray stone. It barely jutted up out of the ground and blended in with all the other rocks that were scattered throughout the orchard, but it would have been enough to send her sprawling if she hadn't caught herself in time.

Alex stopped short.

"This is it," he said, and Evie knelt down, tracing the letters on the stone with her finger.

R-O-D-N-E-Y C-L-A-Y-T-O-N.

"It *is*," she said. It was like making up a story only to find out that each bit you made up was actually true. "Guess I should plant the seed."

"No turning back. Right?"

Evie pulled out the box and opened the lid. A cold gale swirled about them, growing stronger by the minute.

"Something's happening," Alex whispered.

Evie leaned down to dig a small hole, fighting against the whirling wind. Her fingers froze as she dug into the dirt, but finally she turned her palm and dropped the seed into the ground. She covered the hole with the loosened dirt, and as quickly as it had begun, the wind stopped and the orchard grew eerily still.

They waited, straining to spot something that might be out of place.

"Do you think anything is different?" Evie asked.

Alex answered in a whisper. "I don't see any other ghosts, if that's what you mean."

Evie felt her disappointment rising again.

It was just an old seed.

Then Alex straightened. His eyes widened in surprise and he knelt down beside Rodney's grave, staring at the hard ground.

"What's the matter?" Evie asked.

Alex turned to her and grinned.

"The seed…," he said. "It's growing!"

CHAPTER SEVENTEEN

The Tree

o you see it?" Alex asked, pointing at the spot where she'd planted the seed.

Evie looked hard.

"It's right there," Alex said, hopping back and forth from one foot to the other.

Evie squinted at the ground beside the gravestone, but she saw only the hard brown dirt and the dry stalks of grass.

"I...I can't see anything," she said, but Alex shook his head.

"You're looking with your eyes," he said. "You've got to look with something else, remember?"

Evie bit her lip. "I don't know how," she said, but as soon as the words had escaped she knew they weren't true. Of course she knew how! She'd done this with Mom a thousand times.

Her heart beat fast against her chest and she

squinted at the ground. Then she closed her eyes, breathing deep, and when she opened them…

She saw it.

A tiny green shoot was coming up out of the earth.

Evie's breath caught. "I see it!" she hollered, and Alex danced in a circle. The shoot was growing fast, doubling in size in the blink of an eye. Evie felt like Jack must have felt as the beanstalk grew.

She thought of all her mother's magical stories and remembered how she'd told Father she didn't believe in magic anymore.

But maybe magic still believed in her.

The shoot grew as tall as she was, then twice as tall, then three times her height! Already the first thin branches were beginning to sprout.

"It's going to be a tree," Evie breathed, remembering her vision.

"Then I bet it will be an apple tree," Alex said, "but not a dead one. A real live one with apples and everything."

The trunk of the tree grew thick, and each branch blossomed into hundreds of tiny white flowers. Bright red fruit formed before their eyes. Apple blossoms floated down until they blanketed the ground in a soft carpet of white petals. The air was thick with a clean, fresh scent, so different from the earthy cider smell that lingered eerily in the rest of the orchard.

"It's really alive," Evie murmured, holding out her hands as if she were walking in the rain. The air felt perfectly warm and crisp now, like a late summer day just before fall. "There're more petals than there are blossoms, as if the buds are always growing new flowers, even after they've borne fruit."

She reached out to touch the tree trunk but pulled her hand back at the last second. What if it wasn't really there?

"I'll do it," Alex said. "Ghost hands won't break the magic."

He stepped closer and reached out both hands, pressing them flat against the tree. Then he grinned back at her.

"Come on," he urged. "It's solid."

Evie took a step closer and stuck out one finger, running it gently against the bark. It was rough, yet soft at the same time.

"I bet I could climb it," Alex said. He boosted himself up into the branches and spotted a cluster of apples. His fingers curled around one ripe red shape and he plucked it from the branch. That's when Evie felt the first stirring in the pit of her stomach. She could hear Maggie's voice in her head.

"She stared upward as if she were seeing something very beautiful, only Rodney saw nothing. Then she walked forward, and he called to her, but in a blink she had disappeared and no one has seen her since."

Alex had the apple poised at his mouth.

"Wait!" Evie called.

"Why?" he asked. "I've already got it down."

Evie thought of all the stories Mom had read her as a child. Stories with poisoned apples and lies that tricked human beings into disastrous mistakes. She thought of the lost Eve and the warning on the tomb. Which choice was she supposed to make?

Then she thought of Father.

What if she never came back and he always searched for her, just like Rodney had searched for his sister? Or what if Father was happier without her because then he could work outside every day uninterrupted?

Suddenly it wasn't comfortably cool anymore; it was hot. Too hot.

Evie clenched her fists tight.

"I don't know if I can do it," she said, tears forming in her eyes.

Alex just smiled from his perch in the tree.

"But I can," he said.

Then he lifted the apple to his lips and took a bite.

CHAPTER EIGHTEEN

Into the Magic

he world grew suddenly strange and woozy.

One moment Alex was right in front of her, and the next moment he was gone. Evie tried to think clearly, but her head was spinning. All she could see was the tree swirling by in streaks of brown bark, green leaves, white petals, and red apples. The one thing that stayed in focus was a single brilliant apple hanging off a tree branch just beyond her arm's reach. Evie walked toward it.

"Alex?" she called, but there was no answer.

He'd gone ahead without her.

Evie took a deep breath. Behind her the wind rippled through Father's orchard, as if it were calling her back, but ahead of her the apple swayed back and forth.

She had to know.

Evie reached out and plucked the apple from the branch and instantly the tree fell back, a distant blur at the end of a swirling tunnel of petals. Evie held the fruit tight to her lips, and took a step forward into the mirage. She bit into the tart skin, the sweet juice trickling down her throat. Then before she could take a breath, she was tumbling from a height so far up she knew she would fall for a very long time.

At last, it stopped.

The relief was so great she felt as if she had fallen into a very peaceful sleep. Every muscle relaxed and her eyes, which had been squeezed shut, were now gently closed. She couldn't say how long it was before she breathed again. Was she waking up from a long sleep? Had it been minutes or hours?

When she opened her eyes, Evie gasped. She was still in the orchard, but all around her the apple trees were in bloom. Not just *her* tree, but all of them. She was lying on a bed of moss surrounded by hundreds of flowers and a sweeping blue sky above. The grass was lush and green and plants grew everywhere, weaving in and out of the rows of trees.

Where was she?

Evie stood up. The warmth caressed her skin and she breathed deeply of the perfumed air. She turned in a circle, taking everything in.

"Mom?" she called, searching for the spot where

her mom would dash out with hugs and kisses. But it was Alex who jumped from a cluster of sunflowers.

"Now aren't you glad I ate that apple?" he crowed, hands on his hips. He took off the heavy black coat he'd worn every day since she'd met him and threw it on the ground. Evie peeled off her coat, too, and dropped it in a heap next to his.

"Have you seen my mom?" she asked, but Alex shook his head.

"Not yet," he said as he spotted an apple in the tall grass. He chased after it, kicking it around the tree, then straight through the two tallest sunflowers.

"Goal!"

He raised both hands high, and his eyes sparkled in the sun.

"It's perfect here!" Alex said, reaching down to pluck another apple. He tossed it to Evie and she grabbed it without thinking.

"Do you think this is your garden?" Alex asked. "Or maybe it's heaven…"

"I don't know," Evie said. "I imagined my garden would be different—with waterfalls and castles and animals." *And Mom,* she thought, looking around one more time. "This still looks like Father's orchard, only Father could never plant this many flowers, even if he worked his whole life."

They were standing in a sea of them.

"Who says heaven doesn't look like earth, only better?" Alex asked. "Come on," he said. "Let's explore!"

They set off through the apple trees, darting in and out of the center row. Evie watched for signs of her mom's presence—maybe a note left as a clue to a treasure hunt, or a sandal her mother had lost as she ran ahead of them. But there was nothing.

Gradually her pace slowed, and Alex got so far ahead he had to run back to find her.

"I wonder if the trees go on forever," he said, breathless, and for a second Evie felt lost. A wave of hot fear swept over her, but she shook it away.

"We could climb the tallest tree and find out."

"I'll do it," Alex said, wedging his foot into the crook of a tree that looked slightly taller than the rest. He pushed himself up, then moved from branch to branch, stopping only once to pluck a fat red apple.

"Alex, you don't know what will happen if you—"

He bit into it before she could stop him, and Evie held her breath, only this time nothing happened.

"Didn't work," Alex said. "Guess it only works with the apples from the tree we grew."

Either that or we're trapped, Evie thought, but again

she pushed the fear away. Alex had to be right. Theirs was the only magical tree, so of course those were the only apples that were magic....

Evie's thoughts were interrupted by Alex's yell.

"Land ho," he hollered from the top of the tree. "I see your father's truck, Evie, and the cemetery and there's your house. They're not far..."

"The world would be my garden, Evie, my love. The whole entire world."

Was that where Mom was waiting?

Evie took off running, pumping her legs as fast as she could. The tall grass brushed against her as she trampled a path of brightly colored flowers, but Evie didn't care. She didn't even care that Alex was calling for her to wait up. She ran until she burst out of the orchard onto her own front lawn.

She stopped, and her breath caught. The yard was full of tulips and daffodils, and the willow tree that tapped on her window was so wide and full that its branches covered the ground. The cherry tree was heavy with ripe red cherries, and her house was a brilliant white, as if it had just gotten a new coat of paint. The sides were completely covered with tiny white flowers, and the shutters, once a battered gray, were bright blue with morning glories.

Evie's laughter bubbled over. She took a step forward, then before she knew it she was running again, fast as she could, up to the house.

She burst inside.

"Mom!"

Evie dashed from the living room to the kitchen, but both were empty.

"Mom?" she called again, confused. "Where are you?"

Then she paused.

Of course Mom wouldn't be waiting in the kitchen. Her mother had been a horrible cook! And she certainly wouldn't be sitting in the cold, drafty living room, where there weren't even any bookshelves. Mom would be waiting in Evie's room, taking out the paints and setting up the easel. She'd be snitching one of Gram's famous peanut butter cups.

Evie raced up the stairs, taking them two by two.

"Mom! I'm here. I came to find you, just like I said!"

She flung her bedroom door open, the smile nearly splitting her cheeks, but in an instant, tears sprang to her eyes.

There was no one inside.

Evie went out again and searched the entire upstairs, but the house was empty. Finally she stepped back into her bedroom and opened the closet door. She peered under the bed and behind the dresser.

How was it possible that her mother wasn't here? Evie had planted the seed and eaten the apple!

She heard Alex calling below, but she didn't answer. Instead she latched the door tight and curled up on her bed.

What good was a magical world if Mom wasn't waiting for her?

For a long time Evie didn't move, tears making salty paths down her face. Then she got up and pried open her bedroom window. She leaned on the windowsill, resting her head on her arms, listening to Alex's footsteps on the porch below. A cascade of morning glories covered the shutters, and she pulled a string of them inside, stroking their petals absently.

Maybe she'd come to the wrong garden.

She closed her tired eyes, remembering her mother's tiny flower patch back in Michigan. She could still see the morning glories exactly where Mom had planted them—only they'd been the white kind rather than the blue. She could almost see Mom with the watering can, and Evie wished with all her heart that the seed had brought her to *that* garden, back before anything bad had happened.

"I wish I could make everything different," she whispered.

She opened her eyes, wiping the tears away with the back of her hand, then she sniffed hard. She was about to turn when she looked at the string of flowers. The center one was white now, with tiny blue darts, just like the flowers she'd remembered.

"How did that happen?" Evie asked aloud, but she didn't have time to figure it out because Alex's footsteps were clomping up the stairs.

"Are you in there, Evie?" he asked. "If you're playing hide-and-seek, you're not a very good hider, because I could see you run inside the house from the tree. I didn't even need my ghost powers."

Evie unlatched the door, hoping Alex wouldn't notice her flushed cheeks and red eyes.

"What's the matter?" he said, his forehead scrunching up.

Evie shrugged. "Nothing. I thought maybe my mom would be here, that's all."

"She will be," he said lightly, throwing himself onto her bed. "She's probably just waiting around the corner or something. Maybe there are lots of people out there…in town…or…"

Evie shook her head.

"I don't know, Alex," she said. "What if she's still dead?"

"She's *not,*" Alex said roughly, sitting up. "You never believe me, but we're going to find them."

Them? Evie wondered. Who else were they looking for? But before she could ask, Alex spotted the flower.

"Hey, look at that weird flower. There're so many blue ones and one white one right in the middle."

"I know," Evie said. "I changed it."

Alex's eyes bulged.

"You did *what*? When were you going to tell me?"

Evie shrugged. "I didn't think it was that important."

"Not important? We might have superpowers and you don't even care?" Alex bounced off the bed. "How did you do it?"

"I...well, I was remembering Mom's garden back home because she used to grow morning glories, only Mom always grew the white ones, so I was wishing these flowers were different, and when I looked down..."

Alex had already grabbed the string of flowers and was scrunching his eyes shut, crushing the stem between his fingers. When nothing happened he looked up.

"It didn't work," he said, scowling.

"Of course it didn't. I'm surprised you didn't kill the poor things!"

Alex scrunched his eyes shut one more time, but again nothing happened.

"You try it," he said, thrusting the flowers at Evie. "See if it works a second time."

Evie sighed and stroked the soft petals of the flower on the end. She closed her eyes and tried to remember what it had felt like to change the first one. She'd been thinking of Mom, wishing things were different, and she'd wished it so hard that...

This time she could feel the flower change beneath her fingertips, as if a small trickle of life were running through her and she could shape it the way that she wanted.

"Whoa," Alex murmured. He closed his eyes like Evie had. "I'm going to try wishing for something else—like chocolate or an airplane or, no, wait...I'll wish for a million dollars."

Evie laughed, but there was only one thing she wished for. *Mom.*

They concentrated hard, making their separate wishes, but then Alex shrugged.

"Nothing?" he asked. Evie shook her head.

"It's okay," Alex said. "I bet we just have to practice, that's all. Come on," he added, "let's try and make a huge chocolate cake in the kitchen."

Alex bounded down the stairs, and Evie followed slowly behind him, but before she left her room, she turned and took one last look at the perfect white morning glories.

CHAPTER NINETEEN

The House of Alex Cordez

ry as she might, Evie couldn't make a chocolate cake. In fact, she couldn't make anything Alex asked her for. The only thing she managed to change was the spider plant in the living room that had been dying since their long trip from Michigan. She placed her hand on the thin green leaves and wished for them to grow.

"Live," she whispered, and one by one the wilted leaves perked up again.

"I did it," Evie said, grinning.

Alex frowned from across the room. "Quit showing off," he said as the leaves doubled in size, stretching down to reach the floor.

"I'm not showing off," Evie said. "Why don't you quit wishing for stupid stuff you can't have and try changing something living instead? I think it only works on live things."

Alex sighed and stepped over a snaking tendril as

he walked across the living room. "Hey," he said, "you better tell it to stop or it's gonna fill up the whole room."

Evie looked at the plant. It *was* getting rather large. In fact, it had already filled the entire corner.

"Stop growing," she said, but the plant didn't respond, its thin branches reaching out over the carpet.

Alex climbed on top of the coffee table.

"Do something!" he told her, but Evie shook her head.

"I'm trying!"

She felt the familiar sense of life flowing through her as the plant grew despite every command she gave. Then she felt a chill despite the warmth, and this time it was Father's voice she heard in her head.

"There's a time for birth and a time for death. Life moves in cycles, Evie. That's the way things are meant to be."

The leaves of the spider plant covered the floor like an ocean. "Push it back," Alex said as the tendrils rose around him like waves. They surrounded Evie, coming all the way up to her neck until she felt as if she might drown.

Reluctantly she reached out and imagined the plant withering away, and this time instead of the warmth of life, she felt a thin cold sensation running through her veins. Instantly she stopped, but it had been enough. The tendrils retreated back to where they belonged.

Evie shivered. *What had she done?*

But Alex hopped off the coffee table, grinning. "That was cool," he said, studying the shrunken plant. "Let's go to my house next."

Evie paused. "Alex, have you thought about the tree?" she asked. "Who knows how long it will last. Maybe we should think about going home soon."

"Are you crazy?" Alex asked. "There's no way we're going home before I've used our superpowers. Besides, we've hardly even explored. No turning back, remember?"

Evie opened her mouth to argue. She thought about describing the icy feeling that had run through her fingertips, but Alex was already stepping into the hallway and opening the front door.

"Last one off the porch is a rotten egg!"

He took off at a sprint and Evie shook herself, forcing her feet forward. By the time she jumped off the porch, Alex was already in the graveyard, dodging headstones like obstacles on an obstacle course. Evie strained to catch up, every one of her muscles stretching and groaning, and her hair flowing out behind her.

Even with her long legs, Evie couldn't reach him. Alex ran faster than anyone she'd ever met, glancing over his shoulder occasionally to see how close she was. It was as if he were running toward something Evie couldn't see, and she thought that no matter how fast she ran, she would never be able to catch him.

It was only when they reached the trees behind the graveyard that he stopped so abruptly they both nearly fell over. Evie held her side, breathing hard, but Alex dug through the brush until he found the spot he was looking for.

"It's my secret shortcut," he said, concentrating hard. Evie sighed, thinking they might be there all day, but then the bushes parted, clearing a path ahead of them.

"Did you see that?" Alex asked, making a fist. "I knew I could do it!"

He ducked into the brambles and Evie followed, feeling the brush snap back into place at her heels. The branches reminded her of the spider plant and her heart began to pound, but as quickly as they'd gone in they were through, emerging on the other side onto a large, sculpted lawn.

"Wow," Evie gasped. "You lived here?"

The house in front of her was huge. It was gleaming white, covered in the same tiny flowers as her house. There were gigantic pillars and a fountain stood in the middle of a circular driveway. Water shot upward and crested down again, glinting in the sunlight.

"Yup," Alex said. He walked across the lawn and up the steps to the front door. "My dad bought this place years ago so he could escape his job in the city. It's the biggest house in five counties, but it's not usually so..." He frowned.

"Bright," Evie finished, thinking how different her own house had looked. Alex stopped, studying everything as if he were seeing it for the first time.

"That fountain hasn't been on in a year," he said. "Not since I got sick. I used to love watching the water droplets make patterns as they fell. Back then there wasn't anything sad or..."

For a moment a dark gloom draped over him, the way the heavy black coat used to drape over his shoulders, but then it was gone and he turned the door handle and peered inside. He laughed, dispelling the last of the darkness, then burst through the front door, dashing up the huge spiral staircase before Evie had a chance to follow.

"Wait up," she hollered after him, but Alex had already disappeared.

Evie sighed and stepped through the doorway.

"Hello?" she called, but of course there was no answer.

Inside, the house was huge and hollow, like a warehouse. It was cool and smelled of roses. There were chairs and tables, desks and couches, tall clocks and gold-framed paintings, but they couldn't begin to touch the high ceilings and wide windows and long hardwood floors. Evie stepped into the first room she saw, which was a huge dining room with a crystal chandelier in the center ceiling and chairs with red velvet seat cushions around a table. Evie ran her fingers over the soft coverings.

She stepped out of the dining room and moved farther down the hall until she found a large living room. Then she peered through the door looking for someone alive—anyone—but the room was empty. Evie stepped inside and stared at the tall bookcases. She wondered if Alex had read any of these books, but she didn't wonder very long. Instead her eyes were drawn to two giant picture frames, each draped with a black cloth.

Evie tiptoed to the first one and stood in front of

it. She lifted a corner of the cloth to peek underneath, but it was dark and shadowy so she couldn't see. She pulled the cloth higher, then a little higher, until it fell away completely.

There in front of her was Alex. He was dressed in a beautiful suit that made him look slightly older than he usually looked, and his hair was combed, but it was definitely him. He looked handsome, like a prince, poised with one arm on a banister.

"Cover that up."

It was Alex's voice behind her, and Evie jumped guiltily.

"Sorry," she said. "I—"

"Mom likes them covered," Alex interrupted. "It's too hard for her to look at the portraits. That's why we keep them that way."

Evie still held the edge of the black cloth. She was about to try to replace it, but Alex walked forward and traced the outline of one shiny dress shoe with his finger.

"I remember the day that was painted," he said at last. "I had to stand for so long with my hand on that banister, and Mom was cross because I fidgeted too much." His forehead creased as his finger traced another line.

"There *must* be people here," he whispered, shaking his head.

"Who are you looking for?" Evie asked.

Alex glanced up quick.

"Everyone," he answered. "My parents, the gardener, the cook…Where are they?"

Evie had been wondering the same thing.

"I know they're around here somewhere," Alex said. "Maybe they went into town. Do you think that's where your mom might be? I've got an extra bike, so we could ride in." He headed to the door, pausing to study Evie closely. "You're not afraid, are you?" he asked.

Evie frowned, twisting the black cloth tight in her hands.

"Of course not," she said, but it was a lie. A tiny flicker of fear was growing stronger by the minute, and she couldn't help thinking of the tree.

She thought of all the stories she and Mom had ever read, but try as she might she couldn't recall… was there any return once you'd eaten the apple?

CHAPTER TWENTY

Into Town

ust as Alex had promised, there were two bikes in the garage. Actually there were four bikes, but two of them were too big, so Evie took the gold one that matched Alex's. The seat was covered with dust, and Evie blew it off with a puff of breath. Alex peeled out of the driveway, and it seemed to Evie that, again, he was racing toward a finish line that only he could see.

"Are you sure you know the way?" Evie called once they'd been riding for a while. The paved road gave way to a dirt road and the bikes jarred over the loose pebbles. Sweat beaded on Evie's forehead, and she pushed up the sleeves of her sweater but they fell back down again.

"I've done this a million times," Alex called back to her. "It's just ahead."

Sure enough, soon they were at the edge of Main Street, where both bikes skidded to a stop.

Evie's jaw dropped.

The entire town was covered in flowers. The boards that blocked the windows and doors of the empty shops were bathed in waves of color and the street-lamps were circled with ivy. Not even a Beaumont *without* a curse could look like this. It was a work of art, as beautiful as any painting, each color spilling into the next.

"It's amazing," Evie whispered.

"Where should we go first?" Alex asked. Evie looked around and spotted the library. If there was one place in town her mother might be waiting, this would be it.

"There," she said.

Together they rode down Main Street, then fitted their bikes into the raspberry bushes that hid the bike rack, smashing the ripe raspberries in the process.

Alex stopped to taste a few of the berries, but Evie dashed up the front steps and pulled at the library door. It swung open easily, and she waited to feel something—some small spark that would tell her that Mom was nearby—but she felt nothing.

She bit her lip as Alex came up behind her.

"It's so weird," he whispered. "The librarian ought to be sitting right there." He was looking at an empty chair behind a desk in the center of the room. "Want to look around?"

Evie nodded.

"I'm going downstairs," she said, slipping out of the room. She walked down a spiral staircase then past a big door that said, VAULT. DO NOT ENTER. Then she turned the corner into a children's room.

"Mom?" she called, but it was empty.

Evie sat down heavily on one of the small plastic chairs, and suddenly she wished she were seeing the real library, where she could take out a stack of books. Then she'd bring them home and curl up in her bedroom with stories that stayed on the page.

Maybe she'd even make Father read one of them with her.

But what if she never made it home?

Evie got up and made her way back up the stairs, where she found Alex in a small reading room with comics spread out on the floor.

"Isn't this great, Evie?" he said. "We can do whatever we want, and as soon as we find everyone else, it'll be perfect…"

Evie pushed a stray comic book with her toe. "I don't think we're going to find anyone else," she said. "All the people are back home in the real world."

Alex frowned. "Maybe there are people standing

right where we're standing, only we just can't see them." He paused. "It's like we're *both* dead now."

With a start, Evie realized that this was exactly what it felt like.

"Let's go," she said, walking back to the library door. She pulled it open, then stepped outside into the bright sunlight. The fragrance of the air was so strong it nearly made her sick. Eerie silence pressed in around her, and for the first time she realized there wasn't a single sound in all of Beaumont. The wooden sign hanging outside the grocery store swayed back and forth silently, as if on greased hinges.

This new Beaumont reminded her of watching Mom develop photographs. Each photograph had a negative that was the same image in reverse. Instead of black on white, it would be white on black. The Beaumont they'd come from had been cold and gray with nothing living except the people, but this Beaumont was bright and sunlit, teeming with plants of every kind, yet it was silent and empty.

Alex slid up beside her. "I don't want to go home yet," he said. "Let's go just one more place." He spotted Maggie's shop. "How about the farm store?"

Evie looked across the street. The walls of Clayton's Farm Supplies were lush and green, and she wondered if Maggie was there. Did she know that Evie had broken her promise?

Evie hesitated, but Alex was already walking over. She followed slowly behind him, and as they got closer to Maggie's shop, the skin on her arms prickled, and she found herself thinking of the orchard's dark, twisted silhouettes.

Alex dropped his bike next to the shop and pushed open the door.

"Check this out," he murmured, peering inside.

Every inch of the store was covered in dark brambles, thick brush, and reaching vines. "Maybe there's someone here."

He squeezed through the door and Evie propped her bike next to his, then followed him inside. She tried to clear a path but had to push with her hands to find her way. Thorns tore at her skin. There was something angry about the room—something completely unlike Maggie's shop in the real Beaumont.

"I'm sure no one's here," Evie said. "No one could stay in this jungle…"

She tripped on a vine and fell, dust swirling as her hands hit the floor. It was then that she saw the bones. Brittle gray twigs. She scrambled to her feet, backing into Alex.

"What's the matter…?" he asked.

"Look."

Evie pointed, and Alex's eyes lit up. "Awesome!" he said, but Evie shook her head.

"No, it's not. Don't you see? It's Eve."

Somewhere in the pit of her stomach, Evie knew she was right.

"Think," she urged Alex. "Maggie's sister planted a seed, just like we did, and then she disappeared and no one ever saw her again. This room…she must have died here. Who knows how long she lived. Maybe she tried to get home but couldn't make it."

"Or maybe she wanted to stay."

Evie frowned.

"Who would want to stay here?" she asked, but Alex was already reaching out to touch the brittle fingers of the long-dead hand.

"What are you doing?" Evie asked.

Alex was breathing hard. "I get it now," he said. "I know how we'll bring the people back."

"What are you talking about…," Evie started, but Alex's eyes were already closed tight. He breathed deep and Evie felt warmth seeping into the room. A breeze blew through the shop and then a golden light began to glow just where Alex's finger was touching the bones.

"Live," he murmured.

The light grew stronger and Alex's hand began to tremble. Evie remembered what it had felt like to change the flower—as if she was taking in the life around her and shaping it into what she wanted it to become. She knew that's what Alex was doing, only what shape would the bones take?

A distant outline formed inside its gleam. It was like a drawing of a person rather than a real person, yet the drawing was slowly coming to life. Little by little an old woman was looking back at them.

Eve.

Evie couldn't help herself. She reached out, but her finger cut through the light as through thin air. Then a new breeze blew past, and this one was cold, like the October wind in the real Beaumont. Alex's hand shook, and the figure in the light leaned forward. She was staring straight at Evie, her eyes full of urgency.

What was she trying to say?

Her mouth formed words that Evie couldn't hear because the old woman's voice was like the wind. Evie strained to listen.

Was she warning them?

The old Eve looked at her imploringly, and Evie thought she understood.

She didn't want to come back.

"Stop!" Evie said, but her throat was hoarse and Alex didn't seem to hear her. The light grew stronger and the old woman's outline became even clearer.

Then the image of the tree filled Evie's mind just as it had when she'd first opened the box with the seed, only this time the tree was their apple tree and it was wilting. Its branches drooped and the apples were dropping one by one.

"No time," the old Eve seemed to be saying, and now Evie understood.

She glanced at Alex. He was concentrating so hard that sweat was forming on his brow, but Evie couldn't stand it any longer. She reached for the bones, touching one finger to the smooth skeleton. She thought of the spider plant in her living room and took a deep breath.

This time it wasn't life she imagined running through her. The cold raced into her fingertips and the light began to dim. Evie heard Alex breathing hard next to her. She felt the ebb and flow of life between them, the two forces fighting against each other, but it was Evie who won. The last of the golden light disappeared with a flash and Alex fell to his knees.

He turned and his eyes were dark, like storm clouds.

"Why did you do that?" he demanded. "I'd almost brought her back."

"She didn't want you to," Evie said, but Alex stood up defiantly.

"She did *so*. I saw her in my mind and she was saying yes. If I'd been able to finish, maybe we could have brought your mom back next, but you ruined it."

Evie's mouth dropped open in surprise.

"I'm telling you, it wasn't right—"

Alex didn't wait for her response.

"If you're not going to believe, then you ought to go home."

"That's what Eve was trying to tell us," Evie said, clenching her fists. "If you weren't so stubborn, you might have understood. We've got to get back before the tree fades away and we're both stuck here like she was."

"I'm not stubborn," Alex said. "I'm staying."

Evie's eyes popped.

"What?" she stammered. "But there aren't any people here! Why would you want to stay someplace all by yourself?"

"There aren't any people here *yet*," Alex said, "but that's the whole point. There could be. Just think, Evie, back home no one can see me, but here I could bring back anyone I want. I bet you don't even need the bones. I bet if you just concentrate hard enough…"

He shut his eyes as if he might try right there and then, but Evie grabbed his arm.

"You'll turn into a skeleton, just like Eve!"

Alex sighed. "No, I won't," he said. "All my bones are buried back home, and besides, why shouldn't I stay? There's nothing for me there, but here I have a whole world I can make exactly the way that I want it to be."

His eyes glowed, and Evie swallowed hard.

She thought about Alex's parents, but to them he'd been dead for over a week already. Then she thought about all the things that might have made a boy like Alex want to go home if he were alive, like holidays, or learning to drive someday, or playing video games, or going to school, but none of those made any difference to someone who had died, so Evie didn't say them.

"Are you sure?" she asked instead.

Alex nodded.

"I wish things were…different," Evie murmured, and Alex's eyes softened.

"Me, too. I shouldn't have gotten so mad at you," he added. "It's just I was really close, and I knew I could make it work."

Evie wondered if he was right. Would Eve have stayed if Alex had been able to bring her back? Would she have been a real person or only a ghost?

"I have to go," she said. "Father will be looking for me." She paused. "You'll be okay?"

"Yeah." Alex nodded. "This is the next best thing to heaven."

Evie sighed, and for a long time they stood silently, neither one willing to move. Then Evie shifted nervously.

"I'll miss you," she said, and Alex grinned.

"Of course you will. Life won't be any fun without Alex the Great."

Evie punched him on the arm, but then before she could stop herself, she leaned forward and kissed him on the cheek.

Alex's eyes widened in surprise, but Evie didn't wait for his response. She walked across the shop, then out the open door to where she'd dropped her bike. She didn't turn around until she was ready to go.

"Bye, Evie!" Alex called, waving madly from the doorway. Evie waved back, then she leaned forward, pedaling hard and fast.

It wasn't until town was far in the distance that she slowed enough to take her hand off the handlebars and put a single finger to her lips. It was the first time she'd ever kissed a boy, and she wondered if it counted if you kissed a ghost. But maybe Alex wasn't a ghost here. She could still feel the warmth of his skin, and the memory of it made her think that he was making the right decision after all.

He was choosing life the only way he knew how. Now it was time for her to do the same.

CHAPTER TWENTY-ONE

Mom

By the time she reached the orchard the sun was already setting, and Evie could feel the fear pulsing through her. She saw the image of the wilting tree in her mind and wondered how long she'd been gone. Did time move differently here? Had it been hours? Days? Years?

She shivered, wondering if it might already be too late, but another thought nagged at her as well. Had Alex been right about finding her mom? What if she didn't need some dusty old bones to bring her mother back?

How could she come this far and not even try?

Ahead of her, the apple trees swayed, soft and white against the deepening night. She found the center row with her bright red scarf still marking the entrance, then ducked into the orchard. The canopy of blossoms blocked the light of the moon and she walked quickly, darkness pressing in around her.

Then Evie began to run, trying her best to follow the length of the twisting, turning row. Her legs ached and her heart pounded, but finally she rounded a corner and there was the tree waiting for her. Its branches drooped and the apples had almost all fallen, but it was still there.

Evie sank down onto a bed of ferns.

How long did she have left before the tree disappeared?

She thought of Father and wondered what he was doing right then. Had he been searching for her all day? Or hadn't he noticed she was missing? Would he be sorry if the tree faded and she was stuck in this world with Alex?

Then she thought of Mom and remembered the card sitting unopened on the mantel. Now she had a chance to have more than words on a page.

Choices, Evie thought. *The warning had spoken of choices…*

But there was only one choice she could make.

Evie sat cross-legged, picturing her mom. When she closed her eyes she felt the breeze grow colder, but she refused to budge.

"I'll make it in time," she whispered.

She breathed deep, but her thoughts were wild. They sprang from one thing to the next, first thinking of Alex, then Father, then Mom, wondering what she would look like and what Evie would say first if she could see her just one more time.

She tried to calm her mind, but her heart was pounding and she noticed the apple blossoms lay around her like snow. The moss beneath her hardened and the thud of a falling apple made her jump. She pressed close against the trunk of the tree.

"Concentrate," Evie chided herself.

At first she couldn't decide on a single image of her mom to focus on. There were too many crowding her brain—Mom at her pottery wheel, doing the dishes after dinner, teaching Evie's lessons, lying in bed sick without her hair, asleep in the hospital… Then she thought of the way she remembered her mother best—the real Mom, healthy and beautiful. She remembered the way she'd looked when Evie was small and Mom would sit beside her in bed, reading a book in the lamplight.

Evie's breathing slowed.

"Mom," she whispered, "please come to me."

She remembered her mother's tall, graceful form and the feel of the soft skin of her arm. She pictured her spiraled hair falling thick around her shoulders and smelled the incense Mom burned in her studio, which always clung to her hair and clothes. She studied the pink glow of her mom's cheeks and the way her eyes lit up with excitement as she turned the pages of the book. Evie heard the brush of the pages and the lullaby lilt of her mother's voice.

Her eyes grew heavier and the wind became a comforting moan. She might have slipped into a peaceful sleep, but then she felt the soft touch of fingers brushing the hair back from her forehead. They traced the lines of her face, around her jaw, and over her lips. Evie opened her eyes and there was Mom, surrounded by a sweet golden light.

Her mother smiled, that familiar smile full of love, and she was saying something that Evie couldn't quite make out because her mother's voice was the same as the wind.

"Love you," her mother seemed to say, leaning close until Evie could almost imagine she felt her mother's breath against her face.

Then her mom straightened and looked right at Evie.

"Go home," she whispered, but Evie shook her head.

She couldn't leave when her mom was so close. She stood awkwardly and reached out, but her hands went through the image as if through mist.

Her mom said something else, only this time the

wind was louder than her voice and Evie could barely make it out. It sounded as if Mom was saying she should be wise, or brave, or maybe both, but already the light was beginning to fade. Then her mother raised a single eyebrow in a gesture so familiar Evie stopped completely.

It was then that the apple fell into her hands. Evie caught it, and looked up just as the last of the golden glow faded away.

The image was gone.

"No," she hollered. "Take me with you!"

The ground rumbled beneath her, and Evie lost her balance. She reached for the tree trunk to steady herself, but it was already sinking into the earth.

The wind swirled one last time around her, then the last grasping branch was reaching up from the ground and Evie knew this was her final chance.

She held the apple to her lips and took a bite.

CHAPTER TWENTY-TWO

Night Searchers

hen Evie opened her eyes again she was shivering, lying on her back in the orchard, but the magical tree was no longer above her. There were only the spindly shapes of the ordinary apple trees and the barren earth below. Evie sat up and looked around.

"Mom?" she called, her voice scratchy. Night had fallen and Evie searched the darkness, but she knew without looking that her mother wasn't there. She could feel the familiar emptiness—the loss that ached so much it made her chest throb.

"Mom, please," Evie whispered. "It wasn't enough! You have to come back. Let me try one more time…"

Pulling her legs in tight, she closed her eyes and concentrated. She traced every inch of her mom's outline as she'd seen it before, going over it again and again until she could almost convince herself her mother would be there when she opened her eyes, but she knew that she wouldn't. There was nothing but cold wind brushing up against her face.

Maybe I should have stayed, like Alex, Evie thought. Had she made the wrong choice?

She sniffed and ran the sleeve of her sweater across her face, then she stood up slowly. Her body was stiff and sore, and her teeth chattered. She looked around in the darkness.

Alex. Where was he right now? She wished he could've come back with her, but it didn't matter now. He was where he belonged, and Evie told herself that was the truth of things, but it still left a bitter taste in her mouth.

Why did people have to go?

She was so intent on her thoughts that she barely noticed the light in the distance. Someone was calling her name. It was a man's voice, only it wasn't Father's. Then there was a woman's voice near to the first one. Evie ducked behind an apple tree and stood terribly still.

She heard footsteps.

"They're gone if you ask me," the man said, coming closer. "Curse got 'em for sure. I don't even know why I volunteered to come out here at night in this godforsaken orchard. It was Maggie who browbeat me into it."

"Aww, Burt, you've got a hard heart. Didn't you

see the look on that man's face? Now how would you feel if it was your little girl? Not to mention Juanita. Doctor gave her sedatives from what I hear."

"I should think so. Worst luck could befall a person to lose both sons. We ought to move when this is all over. I'm telling you, Lottie…"

"Oh, hush up and give another call."

There was a pause and then the calling started again, and this time Evie was paying attention.

"Adam!"

"Eve!"

There was another pause and the sound of footsteps again, cracking fallen twigs and crunching against the ground. Someone gave a low chuckle.

"Feels silly as all get-out calling those names in a row like that. I swear this is the strangest place that ever existed. Only in Beaumont would two missing children be named Adam and Eve. Like a fairy tale sort of thing."

The woman snorted.

"Adam and Eve weren't from a fairy tale. They're straight from the Bible, which you'd know if you ever went to church."

"I'm just saying it's strange is all. Two little kids lost in an apple orchard and one's named Adam and the other's named…"

Evie gasped. They had it wrong. His name was Alex, and they'd buried him days ago, so why would they be looking for him?

"Hold still. Did you hear that?"

"Oh, Lord, I hope it wasn't a ghost…"

"Hush, I swear I heard something."

Evie held her breath. She shifted position behind the tree and a twig snapped under her foot.

"There!"

"Adam? Is that you? Eve?"

"If something jumps out I'm going to run like heck."

"Nothing's going to jump out. It's got to be…"

Evie stepped into the open. A flashlight beam hit her square in the face and she squinted to adjust her eyes. Near as she could tell there were two people staring back at her—a stout man and a tall, thin woman.

"Are you…alive?" the man asked, and the woman elbowed him in the ribs.

"Of course she is," the woman said, and then she stepped toward Eve. "You're Eve, ain't that right?"

Evie nodded and the man and woman exchanged glances.

"What time is it?" Evie asked.

The man gave a huge harrumph. "Got to be almost

midnight by now for sure. You two have had the whole town up looking for you. Now where's your friend?"

Evie paused. "Alex?" she said at last. "He...he isn't here."

The woman took in a sharp breath.

"You shouldn't say that, child," she scolded. "We don't want to speak of the dead. It's the living one we're asking about. Where's Adam?"

Evie felt like her knees might give way.

"I...I don't know what you're talking about," she managed. "I want to see my father."

The woman came nearer and took off her coat, draping it around Evie's shoulders.

"You look ill," she said. "You've got to be about frozen running around with no coat on in this weather." She turned to the man. "Burt, I'm taking her inside."

"All right," Burt said, but then he turned to Evie one more time. "You're sure you don't know where the boy might be? His parents already lost one son, you know. They were twins even...Now this son is all they've got left. Were you playing together when you got lost?"

Evie's stomach twisted, but she nodded slowly. "We got...separated," she said, because she couldn't think of what else to tell them. In fact, she couldn't think straight at all. *Two sons? Twins?*

Everything was rushing back to her.

Alex racing toward his house, looking for some-one…the two portraits that hung on the wall…the second bike that was exactly the same size as the first one…

The woman was guiding Evie forward.

"I'll keep looking," Burt said. "Least we found one of them."

Evie's feet moved blindly in the direction they were pointed. The woman was following a bright yellow string threaded from tree to tree.

"Didn't want to get turned around out here," she said. "That can happen real easy. This old orchard will eat you up if you're not careful." She laughed, but Evie couldn't do the same.

Had it gotten Alex? Or had he been Adam?

She thought of the figure she'd seen at the grave site the day she and Father had arrived in Beaumont. That aloof, mournful figure. Then she remembered a day when she had been the one at a grave site and all she'd wanted was to go where Mom was going.

There was only one reason she was glad she hadn't stayed behind, and now she wanted to reach him more than anything else in the world.

Father, she thought, *I'm coming back.*

CHAPTER TWENTY-THREE

Homecoming

The old house was completely lit against the black night. Evie fixed her eyes on the golden light streaming out of the windows and forced her feet to take a few more tired steps. She was almost there, but it took all of her energy to make it to the front porch. There were voices coming from inside, and finally Father was opening the door.

For a moment she wondered if he'd missed her, but then he was vaulting over the railing and she was in his arms.

"Evie," he said, his voice trembling, "I can't tell you how scared I was. I thought I'd lost you."

Father held her so tight she could barely breathe, and Evie couldn't help thinking that this night might have ended very differently. Father would have sat up waiting all night, every night....

"Burt and I found her out in the orchard," said

the woman who'd brought Evie in. "I gave her my coat because she seemed half frozen."

"Thank you," Father said. "Thank you so much."

He carried Evie up the porch steps and into the house. People Evie didn't recognize cheered when Father brought her in.

"One more to go!" someone hollered, and everyone cheered again. Evie swallowed hard. Father slipped the coat off Evie's shoulders and handed it back to the woman.

"I'll be going home now," she said. "Burt's out looking for the other one, but I've got some aches in my bones. The temperature's dropping quick. Wish I could stay, but it's been a long night already."

"Of course, of course," Father murmured. He carried Evie into the living room and settled her onto a mound of blankets on the couch in front of the fireplace. The fire was blazing, and when Evie looked around the room, everything seemed the same as it had before she left. Even the spider plant was wilting in one corner.

Father studied her carefully in the flickering light, and his eyes glistened.

The heat from the fire felt amazingly good, pushing away the cold and allowing Evie's teeth to stop chattering, but just when she was about to relax, a police officer came in and stood behind Father.

"I'll need to have a few words with her," the policewoman said, and Father nodded, but Evie shook her head. What would she say? That she'd eaten an apple from a magical tree and seen a place that couldn't exist and that Alex...

"Give her a minute," Father said. "She just got here. Let me get her something hot to drink and something to eat."

The officer nodded, and Father got up as if to go, but he hesitated, looking Evie over from head to toe as if making sure she was all there.

"You're okay?" he asked, and Evie nodded.

"I'll be right back," he said, sliding out of the living room. The policewoman sat down in one of the rockers near the fireplace. She smiled kindly at Evie, then turned to the person in the other rocker, who was half hidden in the shadows.

"Hello there, Maggie," she said. "You're still here, eh?"

It was the first time Evie had noticed Maggie. She was sitting in the rocker farthest from the fireplace, bundled in blankets, and she looked tired and older than Evie had seen her look. Her long hair was loose and it fell about her shoulders. She nodded at the policewoman, then turned back to Evie.

"Hello, Eve," she said. "I've been worried about you."

Their eyes met, and Evie flushed, remembering the promise she'd broken. She wished the policewoman were not sitting right there so she could apologize and tell Maggie the whole story.

Then Maggie's face softened.

"It's just good that you're back," she said, as if reading Evie's thoughts.

Father came in with a bowl of leftover soup and a steaming mug of peppermint tea. He set the tray down next to the couch, and Evie sat up so she could eat. Father sat next to her and brushed the hair back from her forehead. With a pang she remembered Mom doing the same. It had felt wonderful, but Father's touch felt wonderful, too, and Evie wondered how she could have forgotten that.

She took a few spoonfuls of the soup and the police officer glanced at Father, then took out her pad of paper.

"I'm glad you're back, Eve," she said. "I'll need to ask you a few questions, but I want you to know that you're not in any trouble. We just need as much information as possible to help us locate the missing boy. Whatever help you can give us would be appreciated. I saw his mom and dad just before I came here, and they are beside themselves with worry. His mother sits in her rocker praying for his return, and she won't stop even for a moment."

Evie looked down, trying not to imagine that scene. The policewoman cleared her throat.

"Were you with Adam today?"

Evie hesitated. This much of the truth she could tell.

"The boy I was with said his name was Alex."

"Can you tell us about him?"

Evie thought it over.

"He had brown eyes and dark hair that he never combed so it fell in his face a lot, and he always wore a big black overcoat and black pants. I saw him the day of the funeral and he was wearing the same thing."

The police officer sorted through a pile of loose papers in her notebook and pulled out a photograph of two boys in soccer uniforms, one leaning on the other's shoulder. They were both laughing and the second boy was making rabbit ears above the first one's head.

"Is this what the boy looked like?"

Evie studied the picture carefully. It was Alex— twice. The boys looked so much alike she couldn't tell which one she'd known.

"Yes," Evie said.

"This is a photograph of Adam and Alex," the policewoman said. "Alex died almost two weeks ago after a long illness."

Evie shook her head.

"But why would he…Adam…lie about who he was?"

Maggie clucked from the rocking chair. "That's a complicated question, Eve. Sometimes we wish we were the person who died because it's so painful to lose a person we love, or sometimes we think it ought to have been us in the first place."

Father nodded from his place beside Evie on the couch.

"Maggie's right," he said. "I've often wished I could have taken your mom's place." Evie looked up quick, but Father shrugged. "She was so much… better…at life than I am, and I know she would have handled things the right way…with you, I mean. But I guess we don't have much choice sometimes."

Evie sank deep into the blankets on the couch. She wished she could close her eyes and wake up in a world where none of this had happened, but the police officer was leaning forward to ask another question.

"Where and when did you last see Adam?"

Evie tried to think how she could answer. No one

would believe the truth and what good would it do to tell it? Even if the tree hadn't disappeared, she wasn't sure Alex…or Adam…*would* come back.

Then she thought of Father vaulting over the railing and Adam's mother waiting in her rocker.

"We were playing by a tree in the center of the orchard," she said finally. "Then we went into town and that's where I last saw him."

The officer made a note in her pad.

"Did he seem to want to do himself harm?"

"No."

"Do you believe he was thinking clearly? Maybe he was taking medicine or…"

Evie thought over all of her encounters with Adam before they'd eaten the apple.

"He seemed fine," she said thoughtfully. "I wish I had known. If I'd asked him more questions or thought about things…"

She glanced at Father.

"It's all right, Evie," he said. "You couldn't have done anything different."

Evie wondered if he'd say that if he knew the true story.

Father stood up and paced back and forth. "I want to go out and look for the boy."

The policewoman stopped writing.

"You asked me to stay here in case Evie called or came back," Father said, "and I sure as heck didn't want to, but it was good reasoning, so I did it. But she's safe now and that boy isn't. Now his parents are stuck at home just like I was, and no one should have to go through that. There are searchers in town already, and I know the orchard better than anyone."

"Father, don't!" Evie blurted out, but Father just rubbed her arm gently.

"Evie, if that boy is lost or if he's run away from home, I want to find him. Maggie will stay with you until I get back."

Maggie nodded.

"It'll be okay," she said as Father got his coat and his hat with the earflaps, but Evie knew Father wouldn't find what he was looking for.

"If there's anything else you can think of that might be helpful, Eve," the officer said, "this is my business card. It has the station number on there and here's my cell phone number. We'll be out searching until we find Adam, but you can always reach me if you remember something important."

Father kissed the top of Evie's head.

"I'll be back before you're half asleep," he said, but tired as she was, Evie knew she wouldn't rest until he was home.

CHAPTER TWENTY-FOUR

Pieces of the Puzzle

At first the house was busy with searchers coming in and out. There were voices in the hall and the telephone rang nonstop. A man Evie didn't recognize was posted next to the phone, and three times she heard him talking to Adam's father. She could tell because his voice would get very soft and he'd say, "I'm sorry, Mr. Cordez," more times than Evie could count.

Guilt sat like a stone in her gut. Why hadn't she asked more questions? She hadn't even *tried* to convince Adam to return.

Evie stared into the fireplace, where the gloom seemed to be held at bay. She was waiting for the right moment to talk to Maggie, but there were always people around. They'd come in from outside and sit by the fire to warm up, and as long as they were around, Maggie dozed quietly in her chair. Once, Evie even slept for a few minutes, and when she woke up she heard two of the searchers whispering next to the mantel.

"What's even stranger is that Maggie's sister was also named Eve. I read about the family in an article in the historical society's newsletter. Found it when I was archiving. Apparently there was quite a buzz about Joseph Clayton when he first arrived. They did an exhibit of his collection of artifacts at the library."

"Hmph. Do you suppose he killed her?"

"Oh no. I think Rodney did it."

"Rodney? Why, he was only a teenager!"

"Well, it could have been an accident."

"Next you'll be saying this one here killed that little boy."

"No such thing! This would be a result of the curse for certain. You know I saw a black cat go in that orchard just the other day...I'd give a thousand dollars to know what this girl saw. I bet the ghost got him. Her father has been messing with those trees, and if you ask me that's trouble."

"Hmm, yes. Simon tried to give him fair warning, but some folks can't leave well enough alone. Do you think perhaps...Wait, I think she might be waking up."

The voices dropped off, and Evie pretended she

was just stirring in her sleep, but no one said a word after that until she heard one of them say that it was time to head home.

"It's after two in the morning, you know. I don't suspect they're going to find him. That'll make a second one, gone for good."

Evie listened to the feet on the hardwood floor and the sound of the front door opening and shutting. Then gradually the house grew silent. Slowly Evie sat up and opened her eyes.

Maggie was looking straight at her. "I thought they'd never leave," she said.

It felt good to tell Maggie everything. Evie whispered the whole story by the flickering light of the hearth, and Maggie listened in her rocker, never saying much but sometimes nodding and sometimes looking off in the distance and making a low *hmmm*. When she finished, Maggie leaned back.

"That's quite a story," she said. "After all these years it's still hard for me to believe those seeds had any real power, but…" She tapped her fingers, studying the fire. "There are forces in the universe we know nothing about, my dear. Of that much I am certain."

Maggie studied her quizzically.

"I bet you miss your mom even more now than you did before," she said. "How hard it must have been to come back!"

Evie nodded, thinking about her mother's shadowy image reaching out to her through the light. It made her whole body hurt, as if longing was something that used every one of her muscles.

"I do miss her," Evie said. "But I've been thinking about it all night, and I don't think she could have stayed with me."

"What do you mean?" Maggie asked.

Evie paused.

"When Adam tried to bring back your sister, I could tell that she didn't want him to—like maybe wherever she was wasn't so bad. I think it might have been the same with Mom. I know she was happy to see me, and she said that she loved me and everything, but she didn't come back until I really needed her and even then it was only for a minute."

"That's very wise," Maggie said. Then she shook her head. "Poor Adam," she murmured. "I'm not sure where you two went, but I know he can't stay wherever he is."

Evie looked up.

"You said there were *three* seeds, didn't you? Did Rodney give you the last one?"

"No," Maggie said, frowning. "I wish he had, but honestly I didn't know that any of them still existed until you opened that box of yours. Still, the last one must be somewhere."

Evie fell hard against the couch cushions. "What if we never get Adam back?"

"Not *we*, Eve," Maggie said, raising an eyebrow just like Mom used to. "*You*. I may not know much, but I know those seeds don't work for everyone. Whatever magic was in them was obviously meant for you."

"Are you sure?" Evie asked. "Did you ever plant one?"

Maggie nodded.

"Rodney asked me at least a dozen times that I remember," she said. "Once or twice I remember him asking my friends. After a while people wouldn't let their children near my brother." She scratched her chin. "Rodney dated an Eve once, but I'm guessing the seeds wouldn't work for an adult even if they *were* named Adam or Eve. An adult would never believe in the same way a child would…"

"I wish I hadn't believed," Evie said, but Maggie smiled gently.

"But if you hadn't, who would bring the orchard back to life?"

"The orchard?" Evie asked. "What does that have to do with anything?"

Maggie leaned in. "Think, Eve," she said. "If what you've said is true…" She paused. "Remember what you told me about creating life? How it felt? Certainly that life must have come from somewhere. Why else would the trees have died all those years ago?"

Evie thought of Father struggling each day to make things grow.

"Oh, Maggie," she said softly, despair creeping in. "You're right. I'm sure that's why it's so cold and gray here. Eve drew all the life into her world and now Adam will do the same thing, only the orchard doesn't have any more life to give. I should have thought about Beaumont earlier, but all I could think about was finding my mom. It's all my fault!"

Maggie got up and sat down beside Evie on the couch.

"No," she said, calmly, "it isn't. It isn't my sister's fault, either. And it won't be Adam's fault. Pain has a way of blinding us to everything but what we want to see. The only question now is how to bring him home."

"What if it's too late?"

This time Maggie laughed tiredly. "Eve," she said, "one thing you'll have learned when you get to be my age is that there's almost always a way to get things done. You just have to think smart enough and don't take no for an answer. Right now we have to decide where my brother would have put the last seed."

"So you believe me?" Evie asked.

Maggie sighed. "All those years ago when Rodney told me his story I never really listened. I never knew my sister, so it was hard for me to feel his grief. When he told me the story of her disappearance I'd say, 'Enough, enough!' because I'd heard it so many times…But now, listening to you, it's as if I'm truly hearing it for the very first time. So, yes," she said, nodding. "At long last, I believe."

Evie bit her lip.

"I wish Father would believe me," she said. "He'd find the seed in no time, but Father doesn't like stories."

"But this isn't a story, is it?" Maggie said. "It's true."

Evie shook her head. "It wouldn't be true to Father. He'll tell me I was hiding in the orchard and made up the whole thing because I wished it were true."

Maggie let the silence hang between them, then she patted Evie's knee.

"People change," she said at last. "Your father is a practical man, but he believes in *you*, I'm sure of it. Sooner or later, you will have to believe in him, too."

Evie wasn't sure what Maggie meant, but right then the door opened, and Father came in with a blast of cold air and peeled off his hat and gloves. He sank into the chair beside the fireplace.

"We haven't found him," he said. Then he glanced at Evie and Maggie.

"What are you two doing up? You both ought to be asleep. It's after three o'clock."

He unlaced his heavy boots and took them off, setting them beside the hearth.

"I've got to rest, but I'll head back out again early in the morning. There's a new shift out looking for Adam right now. Maggie, you know where the spare rooms are. You can take whichever one you choose."

Maggie nodded.

"Evie," he said, "I'd like to take you with me tomorrow as soon as it's light so you can show me exactly where you and Adam were playing."

"That sounds like a good idea," Maggie said, fixing Evie with a meaningful stare. "There'll be lots of work to do tomorrow, so we might as well get a couple hours of sleep, then you and your father can have a long talk."

Evie nodded slowly. "Okay," she agreed, studying Father's weary form. She wondered if Maggie was right.

What would Father do if she told him her story?

CHAPTER TWENTY-FIVE

To Tell the Truth

"Wake up, Evie." Father was shaking her awake in the dim morning light. "I know it's early, but we can't waste any time. I told Officer Daniels we'd take the next shift."

Evie forced her eyes open, feeling as if she hadn't slept at all. Before she'd even sat up, a flood of memories washed over her—she and Alex planting the seed, the world full of flowers, *Mom*... Then she corrected herself. It hadn't been Alex. It had been Adam. Evie wanted to pull the covers back over her head, but Father was sitting on the edge of her bed.

"Weather's looking like snow today," he said. "In fact, I thought I saw some flurries just a minute ago. Rotten luck, but we'll have to deal with it. Bundle up good. I've set out your long johns and the extra fleece to put under your coat. I want you in two pairs of socks and a hat, and no arguing."

Evie nodded. Father left her to dress, and she

pulled on her layers of clothes then went downstairs to find Father in the kitchen making hot tea and oatmeal. They ate together in silence, then piled the dishes in the sink and left the house, stepping out of the warmth into the bitter cold.

"You lead," Father said. "Show me exactly where you two went."

Evie studied the tree line, then showed him her red scarf.

"We went in here," she said. "I marked it with my scarf because it was exactly the center row." Father nodded and the two of them stepped into the orchard.

"We were looking for Rodney's grave. I wanted to plant the seed there, and Alex, I mean, Adam, told me Rodney had been buried in the center of the orchard. We walked down this row until we found the stone."

Father listened quietly. For a long time the only sounds were the crunching of their shoes and the cawing of the crows overhead, then Father cleared his throat.

"Why didn't you tell me you'd met Adam?"

Evie looked up.

"Because he told me he was dead, and I knew you wouldn't believe I'd met a ghost."

"I wouldn't have," Father said, "but sometimes that can be a good thing. I could have helped you figure out what was true."

Now it was Evie's turn to be silent. They walked until there were only apple trees in every direction and then the ground sloped down and turned and they arrived at Rodney's gravestone.

"We planted the seed here," Evie said.

Father knelt down to study the disturbed earth near the stone.

"Then what?"

Evie paused, but the words she wanted to say stuck in her throat.

"Then we went into town and Adam said he wanted to stay, but I said I needed to go home, so we each went our separate ways and that's the last I saw of him."

Father scratched his beard the way he always did when he was thinking things through.

"So it was right after you planted the seed that you and Adam went into town?"

"Yes."

"What time would you say that was?"

"I don't know because I didn't have a watch."

"Well, was it light out?"

Evie shrugged.

"What were the two of you doing before you planted the seed?"

"Just playing."

"I looked for you at twelve o'clock for lunch, and you weren't at the house. That's when I knew you were missing. Would you say you were planting the seed about then?"

"Probably."

"After you left Adam in town, what did you do?"

"I headed back here because…I wanted to see if the seed had grown, but I must have stepped off the path and gotten turned around, and then…I got tired, so I sat down to rest and when I woke up I heard the searchers calling."

Father's eyes narrowed. He was silent for a long time and she could guess what he was thinking.

"There's almost always some truth in every story."

"Seems hard to believe you could sleep for such a long time," he said at last, "and besides that, Evie, you've always had your mom's sense of direction. Never knew either one of you to get lost." He paused. "So tell me…how exactly did you get turned around?"

Evie was quiet.

"I don't know," she said at last. "I just did."

Father took off his hat and gloves and ran his fingers through his matted hair. The snow was picking up now.

"Evie," he said at last, "I think you know where this boy is. The only thing I can't figure is why you're covering for him. You know what loss is, and Adam's parents want him back desperately. You can see the weather is turning bad, so if Adam is hiding out here, he's taking a big risk. Now if you were an ordinary kid I might think you didn't understand how much it hurts to lose someone…"

Father waited, and Evie stared at her feet.

"You know," Father said after a moment, "while those searchers were out here and I was stuck at the house waiting…well, I thought I'd give up and die if anything happened to you. I regretted every moment I'd spent working when we could have been together."

Evie looked up quick. She opened her mouth to say something, but Father pressed a finger to her lips.

"It's just…after your mom died I figured I could make things better by moving us out here, away from everyone else. I don't know why I thought that, I just did…but once you went missing I was sure you'd run off back to Michigan to your gram's…"

Father's eyes filled and he had to stop and wipe them with his coat sleeve, and finally Evie couldn't stand it any longer. She threw her arms around his waist.

"I wouldn't have run away," she said. "I'd never leave you—not for Gram, anyway."

Father laughed, but it was a tired laugh.

"I couldn't think where else you might have gone," he said, "and if it wasn't for Maggie talking me through things, real calm and steady..."

Father took a deep breath.

"I don't want you to regret the choices you're making right now. Wherever Adam is, you need to tell me. No one's going to get in trouble, and if Adam needs help in any way, we'll get it for him."

Evie drew in her breath. The air was sharp and cold and made her chest ache.

"Father, I...I *want* to tell you, it's just..."

"What?"

Maggie's words echoed in Evie's mind. *He believes in you, and sooner or later, you will have to believe in him, too.*

"It's just that I don't think you'll believe me if I tell you the truth," Evie said at last. "It will sound like one of Mom's stories, and I can't tell you how it's true because I don't know. It just is."

Father dug with his toe through the snow and into the loosened dirt around the stone. Then he stopped.

"You know what the last thing your mom said to me before she passed on was?"

Evie shook her head.

"She said that she loved me, and that she knew I would do a good job taking care of you, and then she held my hand and with her final breath she said one word."

Evie stood perfectly still.

"What was it?" she asked, although she could barely breathe.

Father looked her in the eyes.

"Believe."

CHAPTER TWENTY-SIX

Hidden Treasure

t began with the seed…"

Evie told the story slowly and carefully, with attention to all the small details she knew Father would ask about. She talked as they walked back inside and peeled off their layers, and now they were sitting on the couch warming up by the fireplace. Maggie had made tea and was sipping it in the rocker.

Father listened carefully, his brow furrowed. He didn't interrupt even once. Every now and then Maggie would comment about one piece of the story or another, but mostly Evie talked steadily, trying to remember everything that might be important. It felt like she was telling Father a story, the same way Mom had told her stories every night before bed.

When she finished, Father was silent, staring into his teacup intently. After a while he got up and paced back and forth in front of the fire. Maggie and Evie watched, but neither one said a word.

"Evie," he said at last, "you know I'm a realist. I always have been. I trust what I see with my eyes, and it's hard to believe anything you've told me is true."

Evie glanced at Maggie, and already she could feel the disappointment pressing in.

"But I'll tell you a secret I never even told your mom," Father continued.

Evie looked up. "What is it?"

Father took a deep breath.

"I was always a little jealous of the two of you, telling stories every night. I'd come in from the orchard and there you'd be, sitting on your mother's lap, a book open on the bed before you. 'Clap your hands if you believe in fairies,' your mom would say, and the two of you would clap and clap, your eyes glowing... Sometimes I'd stand in the doorway and watch you there, wishing I could play, too."

"You could have!" Evie said. "We wanted you to..."

Father nodded.

"You're right," he said. "I should have. I don't know why I didn't. But I can tell you this, I'm not going to make the same mistake again. If you need a seed to find Adam and bring him home, then, by God, we're going to find a seed."

Maggie sat up and clapped.

"Bravo!" she said, and Evie threw her arms around Father's waist. Before she knew it, he'd scooped her off her feet and thrown her over his shoulder the way he'd done when she was small.

"If we're going to look for this thing we might as well start at the top. I figure the attic is as good a place as any to find a missing seed."

Father carried her all the way up the stairs, then chuckled as he set her down.

"Bet you thought I couldn't do that anymore," he said. Evie wasn't sure if he meant carrying her or laughing with her, but either one would do.

Father pulled down the small ladder that led to the attic, and Evie climbed up. Dusty shelves lined the walls, and there was only one small window to let in the light. Maggie had grabbed a couple of flashlights, which was good because the snow was coming down hard and steady, blocking most of the window.

"Weather's getting nasty," Father said, looking out.

Evie glanced at Maggie.

"Let's get to it," Maggie said. "I say we start over here. Once we've searched a box we'll set it off to the side; that way we won't miss anything or end up looking through stuff twice. Remember, the seed might be anywhere, so open everything you find."

They opened box after box filled with masks and statues and animal bones, but there were no seeds.

"Papa kept everything," Maggie said. "I remember looking through this stuff as a child, fascinated by every object, but Papa would never talk about his trips. I wish I knew the stories behind everything here, but I don't."

Father set his hand on Maggie's shoulder.

"Maybe it's not too late to find out," he said.

Maggie nodded. They worked in silence again after that, and the searched boxes piled up on the opposite side of the room. Soon, that whole side of the attic was full, but still there was no sign of the last seed.

Father pulled the final three boxes off the shelves, and Evie inspected hers carefully, pulling out carved bowls and old issues of *National Geographic* magazine.

"Nothing," Evie said. Father and Maggie shook their heads.

"Should we look downstairs?" Evie asked, but Father scratched his beard.

"Let's think things through first," he said. "It could take us a week to search the whole house. Sometimes you need to ask the right questions before you can figure things out." He paused. "Maggie, did your brother keep anything in a vault for safekeeping? At the bank maybe?"

Maggie shook her head. "He never had anything of value," she said. "Rodney only had one bank account, and I closed it out after he died. They would have told me if he'd had a safety-deposit box."

"And he never left you a note or anything to give to Evie with the seed?"

"No," Maggie said. "There was only the box. He thrust it at me one day when I was here cleaning up and said, 'This is for Eve, whenever she may come.'"

Father thought things over. "If Rodney didn't have a safe, where else might he have kept something valuable?"

"He would have hidden it, that's for certain. My brother was paranoid in his old age, always convinced the townsfolk were after him. His memory wasn't very good though, so I suspect he would've had to keep something hidden in plain sight if he was going to find it again."

Evie looked up. "How would he do that?"

"Oh, maybe he'd put it someplace where he'd

pass by it every day. Or maybe he'd set something out as a reminder for himself…"

Evie's heart began to race.

"I have an idea," she said. "I know where we should look next."

It was so obvious now that Evie wondered how she could have missed it. But who would have thought to look for anything behind an old painting? Still, it had been staring her in the face all along.

She and Maggie and Father went into her bedroom and studied the portrait of the little girl in the garden. It was done with oil paints and seemed simple enough, but when Maggie looked closely, she nodded.

"That's Eve," she said. "I've seen photos of her, but I never paid attention to this painting before. Rodney must have made it himself."

"It's definitely in plain sight," Father said.

He took the painting off the wall, and Evie blew away a thick film of dust, then the two of them unscrewed the fasteners that held the backing in place. A single weathered manila envelope fell out, and Evie grinned.

"This has to be where he kept the seed," she said. Father lifted the envelope and turned it over. It smelled musty and crackled with his touch.

"You open it, Evie," he said.

"You pick, Tally."

She wished Mom were here, but then she glanced over at Father, and his eyes were bright. Slowly Evie reached out and took the envelope.

It wasn't sealed, or else the glue had long since dried up, so she was able to reach inside and pull out the contents.

A single piece of paper.

"Will you look at that," Maggie said.

Evie turned the paper over, but it was nothing more than a newspaper clipping, yellowed with age.

"It's just a stupid article about the library exhibit," Evie said, remembering the searchers' discussion the night before. "Why bother hiding that?"

Father took the article and read it carefully.

"Evie's right," he said to Maggie. "It's about your father's exhibit at the Beaumont library. Strange thing to keep hidden behind a painting," Father commented. "Doesn't say anything about a seed being part of the collection, but do you think it's possible Rodney never had the last seed and this is a clue to where it's kept?"

Maggie tapped her fingers against the painting's frame.

"It's very possible," she said. "Papa left a good

portion of his treasures with the library before he died. They put them away in the vault, and after a time most people forgot all about them. Papa asked me to honor his wishes and keep the collection there, so I did."

"Do you think we could get to it?" Evie asked.

Maggie nodded, but Father paused. "Of course we'll have to explain why we're asking to see such an old exhibit…," he said, but Maggie just chuckled.

"I think the daughter of Joseph Clayton could find a reason to visit her father's treasures." She looked at Evie. "There's almost always a way to get things done. Isn't that right, Eve?"

This time Evie agreed.

CHAPTER TWENTY-SEVEN

Inside the Vault

The snow was coming down in a sea of huge flakes. Evie was surprised to find it was already a foot deep when they left the house. The three of them bent forward as they trudged down the driveway, leaning against the force of the gales.

Evie was grateful to shut the door of the truck and muffle the sound of the wind's sharp whine. Father turned the key, once, twice... The engine turned over, then stalled.

"Darn it," Father grumbled, turning the key again and again. Evie couldn't imagine trying to walk to town in this kind of weather.

"I'll get it," Father said, getting out and opening the hood of the truck. For a moment he was lost in the blinding snow, but then she saw the hood shutting and Father got back in, shaking the snow out of his hair. He turned the key and the engine rattled to life.

Maggie and Evie cheered, but Father shook his head warily.

"We've still got to get out of here," he said, hitting the gas hard. The driveway was unshoveled and the roads hadn't been plowed, so the old truck shook with the effort of carving its path.

Then Evie had a sinking thought.

"What if the library is closed?" she asked. She could tell Father and Maggie had already had the same idea, but Father shook his head.

"Nah," he said. "This came on quick. My guess is everyone opened up as usual and now they're stuck there."

Evie hoped he was right.

They drove slowly, past the cemetery then onto Main Street, where the store signs blew back and forth in the wind.

"There it is!" Evie said, pointing to the library in the distance. Its light was glowing brightly against the colorless sky.

"Looks like someone's there," Maggie said, letting out a deep breath. Father pulled the truck into what might once have been a parking spot and turned off the engine. They climbed out and the wind and snow filled their eyes and ears. Evie pushed herself forward until she'd reached the front door, then she pulled at the handle, but nothing happened.

Locked.

Father tried the door again, then he pounded on the windowpanes with his gloved hands.

They have to let us in, Evie thought. *Please let someone still be here.*

Then a figure appeared—a young woman with long spiraled hair like Mom's. Evie guessed she was the librarian who'd been missing from the empty desk, and she felt a wave of relief to be in the world of real live people again.

The woman opened the door a crack, just the length of the inside security chain.

"I'm sorry. We've closed early due to the weather," she said.

Evie glanced at Father worriedly, but Maggie stepped forward.

"Hello, Kit," she said. "We're here to pick something up from the vault. If we could just come in for a minute…"

The young woman smiled.

"Oh, hi, Maggie. I didn't see you back there." She undid the security chain, and the door opened wide. "Come on in," Kit said. "Who are your friends?"

"This is Frank and his daughter, Eve. They're the ones who just moved into Rodney's place."

"Would you like library cards?" Kit asked, but Maggie shook her head.

"Today we're here on business. Evie is home-schooled and she's studying many of the places my father visited, so I thought I'd let her take a look at his collection if it's still here."

"You came all the way out in this weather for a look in the vault?"

Maggie just shrugged.

"Well," Kit said, "you're lucky I was here. My husband's coming to get me with his four-wheel-drive truck soon as he gets off work in DuPont. He said it just started flurrying there, but it's picking up now. Strange weather so early in the season, don't you think?"

Evie nodded and glanced at Father.

"We don't want to keep you," Maggie said, "and we're hoping to get back before the snow gets any worse, so…"

"Oh right. Of course. Follow me downstairs." Kit waved them forward, then down the familiar spiral staircase. "The vault's over here," she said, stepping up to the huge iron door with the combination lock.

"I remember this," Evie breathed. "It's like something from a movie!"

Kit only laughed. She had a nice laugh, bright and vibrant.

"Or a *book*," she said, and Evie blushed.

"The truth is," Kit said, working the combination, "other than Maggie's father's collection, there isn't anything remotely exciting in here. We've got some old holiday decorations, but mostly it's full of paperwork."

The heavy door swung open and a stale smell greeted them. Kit stepped in and set the security bar so the door wouldn't swing shut. The vault was a mess and it was impossible to see where one pile ended and another began.

"The boxes are over here," Kit said, taking one down from a line of them. "Which ones do you want?"

"All of them," Maggie said.

"That will take us a while," Kit commented, handing a box to Father. "Why don't you start with this one?"

Father opened it and pulled out a large carved figurine.

"You see," he said, clearing his throat, "this is exactly the type of thing I was telling you about. In our lessons." He nodded seriously, but Father was a horrible actor. Evie would have laughed if she hadn't been so nervous.

"Did Joseph Clayton have any seeds or plants in his collection?" Evie asked. Kit only shrugged.

"I'm afraid I don't know," she said. "This stuff hasn't been on display in years, but you're welcome to poke around."

Through the darkness Evie could see the Halloween decorations and then a rack with a picture of the Cat in the Hat on it. She walked as far back into the vault as she could and studied the boxes lined up on the shelves. There were lots of them. Even with everyone looking, it could still take all day to find something as small as a seed.

Then she thought of what Father had said back home.

"Sometimes you need to ask the right questions before you can figure things out."

Evie wondered what the right questions would be. She stopped and read the labels on each box. CHRISTMAS, ACCOUNTING, SUMMER READING, GIRL SCOUTS, FIRE SAFETY, JOSEPH CLAYTON 5, JOSEPH CLAYTON 6, JOSEPH CLAYTON 8, NOT FOR DISPLAY...She paused. That was a strange label for a box. It was smaller than the rest, too. Then she thought of a question.

If I were Joseph Clayton and my daughter had disappeared after planting a seed, would I put one of them on display?

Evie guessed that she wouldn't. If she believed Rodney's story even the tiniest bit, she would lock that seed away. Slowly Evie took down the box. It was the size of a shoe box, and at first when she lifted the cover, she saw only crumpled-up yellowed paper, but when she pushed the papers aside, there was a stone box exactly matching the one she'd been given by Rodney.

She took it out, and her palms were clammy as she opened the lid.

A warm breeze swirled through the vault, but neither Father nor Kit nor Maggie seemed to notice. Evie breathed out long and full. She poured the seed onto her palm and clutched her fingers tight around it.

Adam, she thought, *I'm coming to get you.*

CHAPTER TWENTY-EIGHT

Not That Kind of Tree

When Evie came out from the back of the vault, the seed was burning her hand.

"Pop, can we go yet?" she asked, using the nickname she knew he hated. Father looked up, and she wondered if he'd understand, but he nodded.

"I suppose these old maps and artifacts will be plenty to get us started," he said to Kit. "Your husband will probably be here soon, and we ought to head out before things get worse." Kit stood up and closed the box she'd been looking through.

"I appreciate you letting us take these things," Maggie said, but Kit only laughed.

"Technically, they still belong to you."

Maggie nodded. "Someday I just might come back to look through the rest. I should have done this a long time ago."

Her voice trailed off, and Evie slid up next to her. Together they followed Father and Kit out of the vault and back up the stairs. Kit found a plastic bag for their things, then she led them to the front door, where they piled on their coats and boots and gloves.

"Maybe I'll see you back again before too long?" Kit asked Evie, unlocking the door to let them out.

"You will," Evie said, knowing it was true.

Then Evie, Father, and Maggie stepped outside into the snow, fighting their way to the truck. The moment the doors were slammed tight against the wind, Evie opened her palm and looked at the seed.

"You're certain this is the one?" Father asked.

Evie nodded. "I think we ought to plant it on Rodney's grave, just like I did before."

Father nodded, then he gunned the engine and stepped hard on the gas, but the trip back to the house turned out to be even slower than the trip into town. In the rearview mirror Evie saw a truck pull up in front of the library, and Kit ran out, but other than that the town was empty and silent and the last few lights were slowly flickering off.

"Hurry," Evie said, but Father was trying to keep the truck's wheels in the grooves they'd made on their way in. The snow crunched ominously, and when they finally made it back to the house, the front wheels spun angrily into a snowbank.

"Close enough," Father said, opening the door so

Evie and Maggie could climb out. "Looks like we're walking the rest of the way." Father started toward the orchard and Evie followed, but Maggie stopped.

"What is it?" Evie asked, turning back.

Maggie sighed. "I'm not so young as you folks," she said. "I'm afraid I won't make it too long out in this weather." She trudged up next to Evie and hugged her tight. "Good luck, Eve," she said. "Whatever happens, make sure you come back."

Evie nodded.

"I'll have the fire going when you return," Maggie said. Then she winked, and Evie watched as she walked away, her form gradually disappearing through the snow.

Evie turned to Father. It was just the two of them now.

"Let's go," Father said, reaching out to take her mittened hand in his thick glove. "Sooner we plant this seed, the sooner we can get back home, where we belong."

Evie nodded, and she was surprised to realize that when Father said "home" she thought of the old house with Maggie waiting by the fire like she'd promised.

She squeezed Father's hand tight.

"There's my scarf," she said, spotting the last of the red fabric hanging loosely off the tree branch. Father ducked underneath and Evie followed, squinting to see through the fierce white streaks of snow. Her nose was running, and soon her pant legs were crusted with ice, and she was glad she'd worn all her layers to keep warm.

She wouldn't have found the spot where she'd planted the seed, but Father knew the trees well. "This is it," he said, kicking away the snow around Rodney's grave with his boot. He knelt down and used his pocketknife to dig a hole in the dirt.

"The ground is probably frozen underneath, but this stuff on top is all right. It's old soil and won't have any nutrients, but…"

Evie put her hand on Father's arm.

"It's not that kind of tree," she said, and then she took off one mitten and poured the seed into the small hole Father had dug. She covered it over and held her breath. At first she felt nothing, but then the familiar wind picked up around her.

"Can you see the seed growing?" Evie hollered when the tiniest green shoot had started up out of the earth. She pulled Father backward so the tree would have room to grow.

"I'm…trying," he said, studying the soil.

"I wish you could see it," Evie said, but Father shook his head.

"It doesn't matter if I can see it or not." He hugged her tight, and Evie watched as the tree grew taller and fuller.

"I hope I can bring Adam back," she said. "What if he won't go? What if the tree disappears? What if—"

Father put one finger over her mouth.

"No more 'what ifs,'" he said. "I believe in you."

The branches of the tree unfurled one by one and filled with blossoms.

"It's almost grown," Evie said, holding out her hands. Mixed in with the snow were the falling petals. Then amid the ever swirling white, she saw the first of the bright red apples.

"It's time," she said, taking several steps forward. Father's gaze never left her as she reached up and plucked the apple. She watched him standing there with the snow drifting silently around him, his brow furrowed tight, but then his face changed, softening with wonder.

"Do you see it now?" she whispered, but Father shook his head.

"No," he said, "but for a moment you looked just like your mom. All grown up."

Evie held the apple tightly. For the first time since Mom died, she felt her mother's presence, not as something outside of herself that she'd brought to life, but as something inside of her—as something she *was*.

She looked back at Father and smiled, then lifted the apple to her lips.

CHAPTER TWENTY-NINE

Back to the Garden

This time the moment she bit the apple and the world began to spin, Evie didn't hesitate. She ran forward into the blossoms. She glanced back once to see Father's form fading through the snow, and then he was gone and she was falling faster and faster, her eyes squeezed tight and her hands clenched, until suddenly she found herself standing in a sea of daffodils. When she turned, the tree was right behind her, fresh and green and laden with apples. Evie wondered if Father was still standing in exactly the same spot, but she couldn't see him.

I wonder if Mom is nearby, too, she thought, and for a single moment she allowed herself to soak in the warmth and imagine the three of them together, closer than her eyes could see.

Then she thought of Adam. Somewhere his parents were waiting.

Evie stripped off her coat and mittens and left

them in a pile, then she ducked under the branches and raced out of the orchard. She found the bike right where she'd left it and got on, pedaling hard. When she reached town she went into every store that was open, calling out Adam's name, but there was no sign of him. The library was locked and Maggie's shop was empty except for the mess of brambles and vines.

Where are you? Evie thought, trying to imagine where she might have gone if she were Adam.

She got back on the bike and pedaled to his house, but when she arrived the house sat silent and still, just the way they'd left it. Evie walked up the front steps and pushed open the door, but there was no sound of laughter to accompany her this time. Instead she walked from room to empty room, looking for any sign that Adam had passed through. She paused in front of the portrait that still hung uncovered.

"Alex the Great," she murmured. "I wish I could have known you for real."

Then she stopped.

In a way, she had. She'd known someone almost exactly like him who'd laughed and teased and balanced on gravestones.

Gravestones…

Evie wondered why she hadn't thought of them sooner. She turned and ran out of the house, down the front steps, and through the secret shortcut Adam had shown her. When she emerged on the other side, the graveyard was in the distance, and Evie could already see a patch of growth that hadn't been there the day before.

She sprinted across the open field.

"Adam?" she called when she got to the edge of the cemetery, but there was no answer. She walked as far as she could until she reached the brambles and pricker bushes that were now woven tightly between the graves. At the center she was certain she would find the stone she was looking for, but first she had to reach it.

There was only one way through.

Evie closed her eyes and concentrated hard, pushing away the life that wasn't meant to be there. She imagined all of it flowing back where it belonged. Back to the real world of Beaumont.

Inch by inch the vines began to retreat, but Evie didn't let her focus slip. She pictured the flowers all around town disappearing and the cherries falling from the cherry tree in her yard and the overgrown weeping willow wilting....She imagined every bit of life that the first Eve had stolen returned to the world it had come from.

Evie felt as if an ice-cold river were running through her veins, but she wasn't afraid. Not anymore.

Finally she opened her eyes.

The graveyard was empty and barren, just as it had been back home, and Alex's stone lay several yards ahead of her. She walked over to it, expecting to find Adam, but he wasn't there. Instead she saw a small wooden heart that said *I Love You* in the middle.

Evie crouched down and picked it up.

It was Adam's sign.

"Adam?" she called. She turned, scanning for the statue of the angel. "I know you're here."

Beneath its billowing robe she saw the tiniest shred of fabric.

Evie hugged Adam's sign tight and made her way to the statue. The angel looked tall and regal, his eyes forever glued on the horizon, guarding the children he'd always protect. But only one of those children could stay.

"If you're playing hide-and-seek," Evie said, "you're not a very good hider, because I can see the edge of your pants."

She waited a moment, then finally Adam stuck his head out.

"What are you doing here?" he asked crossly. "I thought you went back home."

Evie leaned against the gravestone across from the angel. "I did," she said, sliding down, "but I had to come back. I know the truth, Adam, and I won't leave you here."

He frowned. "How did you get back? I thought you said the tree was going to fade."

"It did," Evie said, "but I found another seed. Father and Maggie helped me look for one."

"You told them?"

Evie nodded. "Yup. I told them the whole story."

"And they believed you?"

"Yeah," Evie said, thinking it over. "They did." She waited a moment. "You know, your parents are looking for you. The police officer said your mom won't stop praying for you to come back. And your dad called our house a million times last night when the searchers were there."

"The police are looking for me?"

"The whole town is looking for you. No one's mad. They just want you home again."

Adam ducked back beneath the angel's robe and leaned against its legs. "Well, I'm not coming home," he said stubbornly. "There's no turning back for Alex the Great."

"How about Adam the Great?"

"There *is* no Adam the Great," Adam spat. "There never was." Evie raised one eyebrow just like Mom would have.

"Yes, there is! I met him and he could balance on gravestones, even the thin, slippery ones, and he could run way faster than me, although I'm a pretty fast runner, and he told stories that were so good I believed every word even after I said I wasn't going to."

Adam was quiet for a long time.

"You think no one notices you," Evie said, "but they do." She handed him the wooden heart. "I found this by your brother's gravestone. Maybe someone left it here as a sign for *you*."

"Do you think so?"

Evie nodded. "Yeah. Maybe they need your superpowers."

"You know, I don't really have any, Evie. Alex was the one who could do anything. I wish he'd come back."

Evie blew the bangs out of her eyes with a puff of breath. "I know what you mean," she said. "Mom was good at everything, and I miss her a thousand times a day."

"That's why we should change things," Adam said, "bring them to life, like I told you…"

"But you've been trying, haven't you? And your brother still isn't here." Evie could see only half of Adam's face where the angel's robe split, but his eyes looked heavy and tired.

"I know," he admitted. "Once he was so close I could nearly touch him, but then he faded away. I must not be trying hard enough, only I'm trying *so* hard!"

"You can't outstubborn everything."

"How do you know?" Adam demanded. "Maybe if we try together…"

Evie shook her head. "I already tried to reach my mom," she said. "Just before the tree faded, I saw her for a moment. It was so real…only she wanted me to go home to Father."

"Did she say that?"

"No, but she gave me the apple before it was too late. I bet your brother would have done the same for you if he could have."

Adam laid his head against his knees.

"I can't go home without Alex," he whispered.

"But do you think Alex would want you to stay here?" she asked. "He seemed pretty fun. Maybe a bit of a pain, but…"

A small smile passed over Adam's lips. "He *was* fun," he said. "Alex would do anything, and he never got scared or lost. He always made me laugh, even when we were fighting, and he could tell the very best stories out of anyone I knew."

"Like this one?"

Adam nodded.

The two of them sat quietly for a long while, hidden between the gravestones. The sun was fading and thin gray clouds slid overhead. Evie hugged her arms tight.

"I bet wherever your brother is, he's having amazing adventures. I think he would want you to do the same."

Adam shook his head. "I don't want to have adventures anymore," he said, his eyes glistening.

"But I do," Evie said. "And they won't be any fun without Adam the Great. Please come with me?"

She stood up and reached out one hand, then waited for Adam to make his choice. For a moment he didn't move and Evie wondered if he would stay here forever, lost to the real world just like Maggie's sister. But finally he reached out one solid hand to latch on to hers.

"Okay," he said at last.

Evie grinned, but only for a moment. The

minute her eyes left Adam's they swept across the graveyard toward her house. The walls were bare, and the blossoms in the orchard were already fading away. Dark clouds were rolling in, and the smell of rain was sharp and crisp.

"What's happening?" Adam asked, crawling out from beneath the angel's robe.

"I don't know," Evie said. "I wished things back the way they should've been, but I didn't think everything would disappear so quickly!" She thought of the tree, wondering if it would still be there by the time they reached it.

"We'd better hurry," she said, pulling Adam forward.

Together they ran out of the graveyard, passing her house, where the morning glories had closed and the willow tree drooped. Their feet squished fallen cherries, and a clap of thunder sounded angrily. Ahead of them the wind whipped, picking up blossoms from the ground and swirling them like snow.

Lightning flashed and the ground beneath their feet changed from lush green to cold, brittle brown. Evie looked frantically for her scarf to mark their entrance, but it was gone.

"Which way?" Adam asked, trying to count the rows. He gave up in frustration. "You pick, Evie."

Evie took a deep breath and stood still and tall, remembering the way Mom's voice had mingled with the wind. Only now she didn't listen with her ears. Instead she stared at each of the rows ahead and let her instincts guide her.

"This way," she said, pulling Adam forward.

Rain fell in hard, pounding droplets. All around them the branches were shriveling and the sound was like crackling wood thrown into a fire.

Evie imagined their perfect tree shedding its skin.

"Faster," she breathed.

The ground sloped down and they reached the final bend just as the earth began to rumble. Evie strained to see around the corner, until finally she spotted their withered tree waiting in the center of the row.

"There aren't any apples left," Adam called, but Evie shook her head.

"Look on the ground," she ordered, and together they got down on their knees to scour the glassy grass. Evie was concentrating so hard, she didn't even notice when the pounding rain turned into huge snowflakes.

The rumbling grew louder, making a pit in Evie's stomach. The tree began to sink and Evie lunged for it, hanging on to the trunk with all her might, but it slipped from her grip. Beside her Adam grabbed at a branch and leaned back, pulling as hard as he could, but the ground shifted beneath them and then the last branches grasped upward, like bony fingers reaching out from a grave.

"Mom, help us. *Please,*" Evie wailed, but this time there wasn't a comforting light. There was only the hard ground coming up fast as the last limbs slipped below the earth.

CHAPTER THIRTY

A Tiny Twig

 he last thing Evie remembered was the slam of her body against the ground as the tip of the tree branch disappeared. The air left her lungs in a painful rush, and the world went black.

When she opened her eyes again, she was lying on her back in the thick snow, looking up. Thunder clapped overhead and the world looked exactly as she'd left it.

Except for one thing.

Father was kneeling above her.

"It can't be," she whispered. "There wasn't an apple to eat!"

Adam's head joined Father's.

"Are you all right?" Father asked. "You must have fallen."

Evie reached out to see if he was real, but he pulled her to her feet and wrapped her in a bear hug. He squeezed hard, just as he had when she was small.

"How did we get here?" Evie asked when she let go. "Did you see what happened?"

Father shook his head.

"I only saw Adam come running through the snow."

Adam was looking around, his eyes wide.

"I thought we were stuck there forever, but when I looked around, *there* was *here,* and I saw your father waiting. At first I thought he was Alex," he said, "but he was too tall."

"It doesn't matter how you got back," Father said. "Just so long as you're here."

Evie nodded, but she couldn't stop thinking about the tree.

It's gone, Evie thought, and there were no more seeds left. Then she had another thought. Perhaps someday she wouldn't need a seed to find a magical garden. Or her mom.

But only when the time was right.

"Come on," Father said, "it's too cold to stay out here any longer. Let's get you both home."

Evie took his hand and allowed Father to lead her away, but she still felt dazed, as if she couldn't quite shake the magical world that she'd come from. She stared at the trees around her, remembering what they'd looked like when they'd been in bloom.

Then Evie stopped and drew in her breath.

"Father, look!" she said, breaking off a twig from a nearby tree. "The trees here aren't as bad as the others, are they?"

Father took the twig and turned it over on his palm. He glanced around them at the patch of trees they'd been walking through.

"Well, I'll be," he murmured. "I don't know how I could have missed these." He peered down the long line of apple trees. "I've been through here a ton of times." He paused. "I wonder if there are others hidden away that I haven't noticed yet."

Adam leaned forward. "How can you tell which ones are okay?"

"See here?" Father said, shaking the new snow off the twig. "The bark of the tree is brown. Just like it should be. It's still old, but the outer layer is nearly healthy. And underneath…" He took out his pocketknife and cut open the bark. "The inside layer was alive all along, but the scarring on the outside was stopping it from growing, only now that layer is nearly gone, so the tree will have a chance to live." He paused. "Do you know what that means?"

Adam shook his head.

"Someday we might have apples. I wouldn't have

believed it, but then again I wouldn't have believed a lot of things before today."

Father studied Adam and Evie closely, then he held out the twig to Adam.

"When the apples grow, the two of you will have your hands full helping me pick them. We'll make apple cider and apple pies, and you can bring your parents the first of the early Macs. Can you see it?"

Evie's eyes filled with tears. She watched Father's hands, strong and steady, holding out the twig like a precious gift.

Adam took the branch and held it between his fingers.

"Alex loved apples," he said solemnly. "They were his favorite food."

The laughter burst out of Evie like the pent-up wind had seemed to burst from the box.

"Just like cookie dough and tacos and fried chicken and pizza…"

Adam grinned, but Evie noticed how he clutched the twig tightly, the way someone might hold a secret treasure.

Finally Father nudged them forward. "There will be plenty of time for eating later," he said, "but for now we need to get Adam home to his parents."

"Do you think my folks will be mad?" Adam asked, but Father shook his head.

"Nope," he said, glancing at Evie. "I can guarantee you that mad will be the farthest thing from their minds."

Evie reached out for Father's hand.

"It'll be good to be home," she said.

And she meant it.

A Final Gift

vie was sad to see Adam go. The whirlwind of activity had stopped and Adam's parents had swept him up in a flurry of tears. Officer Daniels had come and gone, and for a while the old house had been full of noise. Now it was quiet again, and Evie thought there was something sad about an ending, even when it was a good one. Her breath caught as she waved good-bye from the front porch, but Father must have sensed what she was thinking.

"I'm sure you'll see Adam very soon," he said, and Evie nodded.

Together they walked back into the house to sit by the fireplace and finish their grilled cheese and hot chocolate. Maggie had even made warm butterscotch pudding on the stove, but Evie only pushed at hers with her spoon.

"What's the matter, hon?" Maggie asked.

Evie looked up. "Oh…nothing," she said. "It's

just I feel bad about your sister. I wonder what happened to her, and why she never came home…"

Maggie put one hand on Evie's knee.

"I guess we'll never know for sure," she said.

"Wouldn't you have wanted to meet her?"

"Oh yes," Maggie said, "very much. But someday I will, and I'm willing to be patient."

Evie glanced at Father and she knew they were thinking the same thing. Patience would be difficult when it came to seeing Mom again, but now they would help each other wait.

Father cleared his throat.

"Snow's letting up," he said, looking at Maggie. "Should we make a run into town so you can get back to your place?"

Maggie nodded. She pulled herself off the couch, and Father stood up after her.

"You want to come with me to drive Maggie home?" he asked Evie, but she shook her head. She wasn't ready to see Beaumont without the beautiful flowers.

"I'll only be a couple minutes," Father said.

Evie nodded as Father and Maggie pulled on coats and hats and boots, then Maggie walked over and kissed Evie on top of her head.

"Rodney made a good choice giving the seed to

you," she whispered. "He must have known you'd be the one."

Evie wondered if Maggie was right. Why *had* Rodney given her the seed? She guessed there were some mysteries she'd never know the answer to. For the second time that evening, loneliness pressed in.

"Mom," Evie whispered after Father's old truck had rumbled out of sight, "I wish you were here so I could tell you everything that happened."

She listened carefully, but she could hear only the howl of the wind, so she closed the door tight and went back into the living room to sit in front of the fireplace. She pulled her feet up under her and imagined how Mom would have listened to the story of Alex and Adam and Evie's magical garden—how her face would have glowed and her eyes would have sparkled. Father and Maggie had asked a lot of questions, but Mom would have laughed or cried and maybe told a story about some time when *she* was a girl.

"I really, really miss you," Evie whispered.

The fire crackled and the orange glow cast shadows against the wall. For just a moment the shadows looked like tree branches, and when Evie watched them her eyes were drawn to the mantel. Then she laughed, soft and quiet.

There was Mom's card, forgotten behind the candlesticks.

Evie got up and took it down, then she tore open the envelope. The card had a single leaf pressed into the center, and the paper was mostly green but there were tiny bits of silver and gold mixed in. Evie held the card for a long time, then finally she opened it, studying Mom's loopy handwriting.

At last she read the words.

My Dearest Evie,

I fear by the time your birthday arrives I will no longer be with you and that makes me so sad. I imagine you opening your presents and wish I could see your face light up! This birthday is one I am especially sorry to miss. There's nothing like an eleventh birthday. Ten is still very young, and twelve is already very old, but eleven—magical things can still happen at eleven.

I suppose that's why I'm finally passing along one final story. I told myself I would tell you when you were old enough to understand but still young enough to believe. It's a story about how I chose your name.

Once upon a time, I met an old man in a shriveled-up apple orchard. It's true, Evie! All the trees looked dead. I was on my way to Claireville, NY, for an artists' retreat, but as I was passing through the area, the orchard drew my attention. I found it so haunting and beautiful I simply had to get out of my car to see it. You can imagine my surprise when I ran into an old man in the middle of the trees.

I think he was as surprised as I was, although when he learned I was pregnant with you he told me he was waiting for a girl to be born who would be strong and brave and wise to bring the trees back to life, and that if I believed my daughter would be each of those things, I should name her Eve.

"Couldn't she be strong and brave and wise if I named her Jennifer or Dawn or Amanda?" I asked.

"Yes," he said, "but then she cannot be the one."

I laughed at the time and went on to my retreat. I never did tell your father about the old man, although I did tell the old man about your father. I told him maybe it wasn't a little girl who would bring the orchard back to life but a grown man who would work very hard every day. I gave him our number just in case he ever wanted to sell the place.

I have to tell you, Evie, I never stopped thinking about those haunting trees and that strange old man. When you were born your father and I planned to name you Grace after your grandma—a very practical name—but when the nurse brought you to me in the hospital and I held you in my arms, I thought, "She is the one. My one and only."

So I named you Eve.

Father wasn't too pleased that I'd changed my mind, but I told him the name made me think of a beautiful garden, so he agreed to it. I never went back to that orchard after you were born. I always meant to, but New York is a long way from Michigan. But I did paint a portrait of the old man, and I sent it to him with a note. I didn't hear from him until last week when he called me out of the blue. He was sad to hear that I was ill, but when he asked how you were, I told him you were everything I knew you would be.

I told him you were strong and brave and wise, and that I hoped you would have many adventures in your life even if I wasn't here to share them with you.

I do wish that, Evie.

I hope you find magic around every turn, and that you and Father will share it together. Remember there are many kinds of magic—there's the magic of trees that grow and birds that fly and there's the magic of growing up and getting older, but mostly there's the magic of love, which cannot be contained, not even by death.

I'll always love you. Happy eleventh birthday.

Mom

Evie sat for a long time, completely still, then finally she got up. She walked out to the hallway and stood in front of the portrait of Rodney.

His eyes were full of expectation, but something else as well.

Adventure.

They were eyes that Mom had painted. Evie reached out and touched the surface of the painting, then she leaned in close and studied the bottom right-hand corner.

T.L.A.—*Talia Lauren Adler*

She stepped back and let out her breath.

Magical things can still happen at eleven.

Acknowledgments

Many times I've heard authors thank their spouses in glowing terms, referring to their undying patience and support. I now know that what they say is true: Being married to a writer is a job for a saint. Fortunately, I'm married to one. Whether it's putting up with the long hours and sacrificed weekends, being sympathetic to my fears and complaints, offering suggestions, or providing a listening ear, my husband has not failed me. I am so thankful for his presence in my life.

I am also very grateful to my editor, Kathy Dawson, who has gone above and beyond for this book. She hasn't merely edited (as if that isn't enough!); she's been a companion along the path, seeing potential at times when I could see none.

My agent, Ginger Knowlton, is my rock, and I'm grateful for all that she does. Allyn Johnston, Tracy Marchini, Beth Barton, Gretchen Hirsch, and Robin

Cruise all provided key feedback when I needed it most. Bruce Cantley and Jeff Crist were invaluable in researching the story. Emily Paulsen was a fabulous role model for Maggie, and, as always, my parents, William and Linda Going, have been a constant source of support and inspiration.

I'd also like to offer my gratitude to God, source of all stories, creator of life, and hope for the future.